THE ARCHIVE OF
ALTERNATE ENDINGS

THE ARCHIVE OF ALTERNATE ENDINGS

A NOVEL

LINDSEY DRAGER

DZANC
BOOKS

5220 Dexter Ann Arbor Rd.
Ann Arbor, MI 48103
www.dzancbooks.org

Library of Congress Cataloging-in-Publication Data

Names: Drager, Lindsey, author.
Title: The archive of alternate endings / Lindsey Drager.
Description: First edition. | Ann Arbor, MI : Dzanc Books, 2019.
Identifiers: LCCN 2018051982 | ISBN 9781945814822
Classification: LCC PS3604.R335 A88 2019 | DDC 813/.6--dc23
LC record available at https://lccn.loc.gov/2018051982

First US edition: May 2019
Interior design by Michelle Dotter

Printed in the United States of America

10   9   8   7   6   5   4   3   2   1

CONTENTS

A NOTE ON HALLEY'S COMET

Halley's Comet is visible from Earth every seventy-five to seventy-nine years. Based on confirmed sightings that extend as far back as 240 BCE, this book tracks and imagines sightings that occurred (and will unfold) during the years 1378–2365.

THE ARCHIVE OF
ALTERNATE ENDINGS

| 1378 | 1456 | 1531 | 1605 | 1682 | 1759 | **1835** |
| 1910 | **1986** | 2061 | 2136 | 2211 | 2286 | 2365 |

OF BREADCRUMBS AND CONSTELLATIONS

WHEN THEY WERE IN their mid-twenties, studying at the University of Marburg, the Grimm brothers—Jacob and Wilhelm—shared a bed. They were offered two beds but chose to share one. They would often retire for the evening together, and when they were ready to invite sleep, the sheets distributed evenly around them, Jacob would say, Yes? And Wilhelm would say, Right. And Jacob would put out the candle.

It was then that Wilhelm Grimm would think of his brother. He would think of his brother and the bodies for whom his brother longed. He would think: if he could tell his brother everything he has learned, it would read like a very sad primer. That soft arcs are deceptive, in stories or on paths. That nothing in this life is unbent, and as such all things intersect. That the sky is a projection of everything that lives within our frames. That there is no closer bond than that between siblings because they derive from the same cosmic formula and grow in the same flesh home.

Right now, a decade after their university days, a woman sits at the table in the home Wilhelm and Jacob have made together. This is one in a long procession of women whom they have hosted in the last few months. The task set before them is to solicit from the women the tales that have defined their country and culture, the tales that are going extinct. The women know the stories best, for they are the primary narrators. These are women for whom work means labor: tending garden, cooking dinner, raising children, cleaning house. Telling tales, the women inform Jacob and Wilhelm, helps to pass the time.

The stories are about greed, lies, abuse, and rape. The stories are about power and despair. There are riddles and traps. There are monsters and ghosts and broken bodies—missing arms and severed legs and lost heads. And, too, Jacob notices, while Wilhelm concentrates on the plot and characters, searing into his mind what unfolds, nearly all the characters enter, exit, or find themselves lost in the woods.

So far their task has been simple. While a narrative might stray a bit in one telling, or embellish or neglect a detail in another, they've received and recorded the stories without substantial disagreement. But now, in this moment, a woman sits in front of the Grimm Brothers, telling them a story of siblinghood that confuses them. Hers is a story the brothers have heard, but this woman's version seems to go astray.

Until now, the narrative of Hansel and Gretel has been a malleable myth, a floating narrative that morphs depending on the kind of hill upon which the country folk make their homes. But this woman is saying that in her territory, the story has nothing to do with famine or being lost. She is suggesting that the children are abandoned in the wood not because their parents cannot feed them, but because the brother is morally wrong.

These men don't seem to understand, the woman thinks. These men, the woman thinks, seem resistant to this version of the story. But she considers it her duty to make sure they've heard this tale precisely because she has come to know that no other region tells it this way. And she now understands that if she doesn't tell and insist that they listen, this version may go unheard. Though she cannot read, she knows well that what gets committed to the page, what gets translated into the code of letters and locked in the coffin of a book, becomes truth while everything else dissolves into the abyss of history lost.

This is why, when the brothers ask what she means by morally wrong, she does not hesitate to disclose the element on which the narrative's crux rests. The story, she says, is about a sister who wants to save her brother. The woman says: The story is about a boy who loves boys and the parents who abandoned him because of it.

The brothers look at one another, trying not to disclose what unfolds in each of their minds. Jacob thinks: Risk. Wilhelm thinks: Jacob.

The woman tells them she's happy to return should they need to hear the tale again. But Wilhelm confirms that their method of collecting is sound. So far it has been: the brothers listen, then record by hand independently, share their record, and combine it into a single draft.

As the woman leaves, she thinks of her son at home. For she knows how this will end: there will be no story for him in the brothers' collection of tales.

The Brothers Grimm sit alone that evening, passing a wine bottle back and forth. Their work is to capture and archive the tales of their community and culture. The question here is one they haven't yet been challenged with: is the story the woman tells the origin, and all the other versions derived from it? Or is this woman's story an anomaly, the original tale contaminated by her line of tellers?

What Jacob does not know is that Wilhelm saw the look on Jacob's face as the tale was being told; Wilhelm saw the way the skin flushed and the eyes grew wide with possibility, and in that moment, Wilhelm found confirmation of what he'd long known: that the story of the boy's transgression parallels his brother's own. He knows well the first rule of storytelling: that all stories—fact or fiction—come first from somewhere real.

Wilhelm thinks about his brother, the person with whom he is closest in the world, the person to whom he tethers himself. He thinks of his brother as his life mate; he thinks of himself as merely one half of what constitutes them. He thinks about how well he knows this man across the table, how they have shared everything: a bed, an education, debt and disappointment, a passion for their country, a womb. Wilhelm helps himself to his brother's mug, takes a long drink of Jacob's wine. He rises and puts his hand upon his brother's shoulder, pats him twice. He tells his brother to sleep on it and they will come to a conclusion in the morning.

And they do. And Wilhelm realizes his brother will not share with him the secrets he keeps hidden in his heart. And many months later, Wilhelm proposes marriage to one of the women who shared with them her tales, and the two have many children. And Jacob lives in the house with them, forever a bachelor and a scholar. And the story of Hansel and Gretel goes like this: two weak and hungry children, a bad witch, and a resolution where the children go home. And it lives that way forever after.

...

Wilhelm Grimm will have a son who will father a daughter who will mother a son who will become a writer and find himself in New York City in 1986. The writer will not know he is a descendent of a Grimm, nor will he know that his Great-Uncle Jacob preferred men, just like him. One day the writer will visit the theatre and catch the eye of a man whom he will take home for the night. They will light candles and know each other together but separately because there is a dark something moving through the love that's shared by men. Afterward, the man will bite his thumbnail as he tells the writer he is a computer programmer. He'll scan the shelf behind the writer's bed and ask to have the writer's illustrated copy of *Hansel and Gretel.* What if I want to see you again? the writer will ask the man. The man will stand, naked, holding up the book. Follow the breadcrumbs back.

Two months later, the writer will pour himself a cup of coffee and open the newspaper, where he will see in the obituaries a photo of the programmer he had invited home just weeks before. He will cut it out and post it to the wall of his studio, where he is running out of room. He will get unsteady looking at the wall. When he opens his window to let in fresh air, the obituaries flutter and wave.

He is thinking: How do I begin to build a structure around this loss? How do I reshape my world around the grid of their absence?

The writer is thinking: How does one narrate when faced with a story for which there is no language?

In his autobiography, Jacob Grimm will write: "Sparseness spurs a person to industriousness and work, keeps one from many a distraction." Jacob thinks of the siblings, Hansel and Gretel, as he lies in bed the evening he and his brother hear the woman's strange tale. The woods, he knows from listening to the stories, are a space of possibility—they harbor the unknown, but they also invite the rush of risk. How the woods draw him, he thinks, lying in his bed at night. Lying in his bed at night, he thinks: how the woods plea.

The illustrated copy of *Hansel and Gretel* was purchased by the writer at a bookstore, five years before he gave it to the programmer. He had opened the book and found himself deeply moved by the illustrations—somehow both gothic and whimsical, relaying both the danger of being a child and also the wonder and awe. The writer paid for the book and put it under his arm; the writer brought it home and put it on his shelf. He made himself a cup of coffee and picked up the paper, where he read a short article about a rare cancer taking the lives of gay men.

The programmer who is given the illustrated copy of *Hansel and Gretel* by the writer will sit down with it one afternoon before he knows he's sick. He will sit in a loveseat across from his brother, who has come over for dinner. The man's niece and nephew will join him, snuggle into his side to hear the telling of the tale. The man will think their forms are so tiny, their hearts beat almost too fast. They are hummingbirds, warm and small and compelled by chance. Hansel and Gretel, the man will say to his niece and nephew, and he will bite his thumbnail and open the cover of the book. Hansel and Gretel, he will read on the title page, and it is then his niece will ask who authored this tale.

The problem, the Brothers Grimm think in their bedrooms the night they hear the story of the abandoned siblings, has to do with silence. Should they tell it as they heard it, Hansel led into the woods because his parents don't want to raise a boy who loves boys, or should they let it dissolve into the waste of the past? Jacob will think: What is at stake in sharing this story? And Wilhelm will think: What is at stake in leaving this story untold?

The illustrated copy of *Hansel and Gretel* will be shelved again after the man tucks in his niece and nephew. He'll feel warm inside, the way it feels to know you share blood with those around you. The man will sit on the couch next to his brother, and his brother will say, You've got to stop being so picky. There is no perfect woman—at your age, you'll be lucky to find one who satisfies half your needs. Find one who is good, marry her, and get yourself some kids.

Before the illustrated copy of *Hansel and Gretel* is bought by the writer—before it is shelved by the bookstore clerk, before it is produced in mass at a factory, before hundreds of copies are shipped across the world—it will be illustrated by a woman in a warm city on a coast. She will be sitting in a hospital courtyard sketching and she will overhear a woman tell her daughter the tale. She will sketch and listen and let all else escape her mind. She will listen and remember what it meant to be a child, when all stories were shared events. Now reading is a solitary venture. She will listen and see through the veneer of a cautionary tale into the dark notions below: the danger of the woods, the parents abandoning the children, the heat of the oven, the trap of the house made of sweets. And when the mother's story is over and she and her daughter rise to leave the courtyard, the illustrator will stop working and realize she has turned the landscape before her into a lush and haunting entrance to a forest, before which the figures of two children stand, holding hands.

In his room at night, in the mirror, before they've recorded the tale, Wilhelm thinks about what it means to narrate. Is there a way to tell that pays credence to the voices that carried the story?

In his room at night, in the mirror, before they've recorded the tale, Jacob thinks about what it means to desire. Does it require participation, or can it surface more covertly, realized but dormant, carefully concealed?

The illustrated copy of *Hansel and Gretel* will live on the shelf next to the programmer's telephone book. After he gets the test results, he will take both books from his shelf. He will sit at his kitchen table and make a list of all the lovers he's had in the last month. For some, he'll remember the last names, but not the first. For some, he'll remember the first names but not the last. For several, he'll know he chose not to know their names at all. He'll make the list as best he can, the page riddled in question marks. Of those names he can't remember, he will know one was a dentist, another a painter, one worked in politics. In the city, there had been a dancer. And of course, the writer. The writer had told him that the fuzz on the small of his back was as soft as velvet. The writer had told him that his neck smelled of summer rain. The writer had told him that, and he had told the writer this: follow the breadcrumbs back.

In his autobiography, Jacob will write: "The imagination knows how to decorate and enliven bare and empty places."

In his autobiography, Jacob will write: "All this never hurt me."

The illustrated copy of *Hansel and Gretel* will be missed by the writer only once, when he wants to reference something he thought he remembered from the epilogue. The night before the writer finds the programmer's obituary in the paper, he will look for the book on his shelf and only then remember. He will smile at the ground, recalling that night. He will smile at the ground and think about the pleasure of the woods.

The trick, Wilhelm thinks in his room, the night before they've recorded the tale, is all about transmission—how to carry the tale forward while still acknowledging the voices that carried it this far. For a story to enter the domain of tale, it must have been through many mouths, passed through generations and across great distances. The story must move through many bodies and get shaped, become taut and succinct through those bodies, perfecting and honing its shape. Does the story reach this final state ever, or is its final state the malleable form in which it never calcifies?

The trick, Jacob thinks in his room, the night before they've recorded the tale, is all about suppression—how to keep the yearning carefully contained. He once thought it had to do with disregarding, but he knows now it's better to permit his desire space to breathe. Can a man live his whole life resisting his pleasure, or are we as a species condemned to bend toward our want?

Meanwhile, the sky loiters above, watching these pasts and futures unfold below: a great and angry storm in the sea, a fight between scores of men who disagree about minor things, a plague spreading through a country and beyond. The sky watches the bodies in the world below fight and fear. There, a child running away from home. There, a woman pushing a baby from between her legs only to learn it is not living. There, a dying man who loves his niece and nephew revealing to his brother who he is, and the brother shutting and locking his door.

Long after they decide how the tale will be told, long after the tale is recorded for the first time, but before the second and definitive edition of the text is put into print, the Brothers Grimm look up at the sky. When Wilhelm looks up, he sees a future—a world in which his children and his children's children share the stories he and his brother record. When Jacob looks up, he sees a future—a world in which he is not made to be silent about his desire.

Before he has an obituary that is tacked to the writer's wall, the programmer who is given the illustrated copy of *Hansel and Gretel* will drive to the South. He will drive to the South because he has heard there is a woman taking in people living with this illness. He will pack his things, which includes the illustrated copy of *Hansel and Gretel*, and he'll drive. He does not know it yet, but the woman will tend him until the end. And after that, the woman will call his brother and ask if he wants the body, and the man's brother will say no. The woman's daughter will be listening to the phone conversation as she pulls from the shelf the illustrated copy of *Hansel and Gretel*. She will not know much about being an adult and even less about being a parent, but she'll know a great deal about being someone's child. When she tries to imagine her family abandoning her, the thought will grow around her like a net of dread. She will listen to her mother on the phone and finger the inked figures on the page, hands clasped at the entrance to the woods.

The night before Wilhelm's wedding, he and his brother finish their last meal together in the house alone. As the meal draws to a close,

Wilhelm takes a large sip from his brother's wine. He puts his napkin down upon the table and folds his hands. Then he says this: If you desire uncommon lips, I hope that you would tell me.

The blood runs from Jacob's face and he permits his body a minor, nearly undetectable waver, but Wilhelm knows him enough to see. Jacob recovers quickly because his life is so sutured to appearance. And Wilhelm places his hand upon his elder sibling's, squeezes it thrice, and rises to go to bed for the last time without a wife.

The man will drive to the woman in the South. The drive will be long and dark and quiet. He will drive through the woods and he knows where the path will lead. He will grow ever closer to the woman and her place of care and rest. The man will think that this will be his last trip across the country. He has seen so little of it, having spent his life in the urban forest. He will glance toward either side of the road, where the woods are thick, glance back and forth until he is overcome. He will grip the wheel and think of his niece and nephew and grow overwhelmed enough to begin weeping. The man will unburden himself with such force that he will not see, and so he will pull over. Then, parked on the shoulder of the road and surrounded by forest, he will get out and stand in the middle of the road and look up to the sky, trying to still time. The man will wait, at first patiently, because to look at the sky means to diminish the problems in his mind. The man will think: My body is on this earth, and soon it won't be. The man will think: How will everything end? It will be a clear night, and he'll try to view the whole skyscape, come to realize just how much the human body isn't made to see. For example, the whole night or our own faces. It must be some trick to make sure we can't bear witness to too much.

The illustrated copy of *Hansel and Gretel* contains an epilogue that very few people will ever read. At the back of the book live these words: "We cannot know how Jacob Grimm desired, but we also do not perceive the great force keeping our feet on Earth. Longing, like gravity, takes work to detect."

In the sky, a glowing rock propels itself through the years, learning the way stories grow, calcify, and dissolve. It looks on, thinks: What of the bodies who home on the rock of that world? What of the bodies who craft their lives around the logic of the orbit? They must not know the first law of their sphere: that they are never gone, but just eclipsed.

In the sky, realms disband.

In the woods, two men kiss.

Read more closely: there are breadcrumbs everywhere.

1378 1456 1531 1605 **1682** 1759 1835

1910 1986 2061 2136 2211 2286 2365

CIRCUMNAVIGATIONS

BECAUSE SHE KNOWS WITHIN her there lingers something unfamiliar and perverse, something at the limits of dread, Edmond Halley's niece fears for her future. This is Caius, France, 1682, and the girls in the village suspect she is in error. When the long days come to a merciful close and she rests her face against the rough fabric of her pillow, she imagines the worst: that she is put on trial and accused, as so many others have been. It must be in her flesh, the costume that covers her frame. It must be in the way the skin wraps itself around its bone scaffolding. It is moments like this when her breathing grows difficult, as she imagines the ways her spirit will be taken from her body: by hanging or by stoning, by burning at the stake. It is a fate she has seen unfold for other women, and even some girls. It is at night, in bed, her face grazing her pillow, her braids unknotting as she turns and rolls her head, that she remembers there is no such thing as a witch, that when those women confess or declare they are one, it is a much more haunting force compelling them to speak. And it is this force she fears at night, listening to her brother's soft breathing. Not that she will be accused, but that she will be compelled to believe.

The comet that will come to be known as Edmond Halley's is coming tonight, but it is not yet his. No one knows that after it breaks through the blank sky this evening, it will curve around the sun, retreat to the far edge of the galaxy, then follow its orbit back.

Four lifetimes later, a woman on the coast of the U.S. will sketch an image in the courtyard of the Asylum for Women, the place where she resides. This is Savannah, Georgia, 1910, and she is an illustrator whose work has been displayed across the world. Her method is pointillist—she renders images through short strokes that, given distance, become unified like the pixels on a screen. She will sit in the courtyard of the asylum, having just been given four hours of hydrotherapy, strapped to the tub by her limbs. She will sketch the image of the comet that is coming tonight, the skin of her hands puckered and wrinkled from the cold water.

Edmond Halley's niece is lying in bed. In the bed next to her lies her brother. They can hear their uncle downstairs, speaking to their father. Their uncle is someone who matters—he got out of the family trade. At supper, he told them his latest theory about what unfolds deep inside the Earth. Beneath our feet are many layers of thin shells, he explained. And below those shells lives an empty core, a hollow inside which anything could unfold. Her brother asked what hovers there, and Halley smiled, looked at his niece, and told his nephew to ask her. Your sister, her uncle said, is a visionary. Her peculiar stories have perplexed me for years. She knows and she will tell you, her uncle said, and he gave his niece a wink.

Now, her brother lies in the bed next to her, sleeping soundly. She can hear her uncle and father downstairs talking, and when their voices grow suddenly loud and then break into laughter, the house seems to shift.

There is a loud inhale of breath and then a muddled cough, followed by rasping. Her brother has just enough breath to call for her. She can hear the fear in his voice and knows from where it comes. He tries to stutter something she can't understand. Take a breath, she whispers, and squeezes his shoulder to tell him she's there.

She has taught him to lock his worry deep in his brain, tend it like a garden. If he can keep it organized and ordered, it does not get out of hand. But when the world grows suddenly larger and more vast than he had previously thought, as when he learns something new—like the fact that color is merely light reflected, like the fact that vapor and ice are one and the same, like the fact that beneath the surface of the earth might be a society of other beings—the fear returns.

Was it the old dream? she asks him. His eyes are wide with wonder, concentrating on his breathing, but he is able to nod. She knows what has unfolded here, as it has for several months. The dreams concern her and her fate, all the ugly ways she'll end. He spares her the details, but she can feel the fear through his thin frame. I will be fine, she tells him. Nothing is going to hurt me. She wipes the sweat from his forehead with the sleeve of her nightgown.

Four lifetimes later, the illustrator sits in the courtyard of the asylum, sketching. A nurse is watching her face as she works. There is a smudge of pencil lead along her forehead where her finger, charcoal-covered, moved a bit of hair. There is the regular twitch of her cheek to keep her glasses from sliding down her nose. The illustrator is sketching and her hair—cropped short for maintenance and wet from the therapy bath—is getting wild in the humidity. She moves across the page, over and over in short bursts to make the comet's tail, and her hand looks frantic, a being separate from the rest of her.

The nurse knows the woman's story, as she has known all the others—women abandoned by husbands, brothers, sons. This woman was once a great artist. She lived in a commune with other artists, and there she experienced long evenings of wine and women and the exhilaration of invention. That was her life until her father—someone unimportant, but with enough money to matter in limited circles—learned about her lifestyle. Worried about his reputation, he put her here. This is a story not unlike hundreds of others, but for this woman, the nurse feels especially raw.

The nurse looks over her shoulder and then looks around the lawn, takes in the other women that occupy this place. It is only by some miracle that the nurse is not inside herself, given her particular transgressions. It is a fact of these asylums that there are more perfectly healthy women inside than women who are unwell. And it is also a fact that once inside, the women who are put here do not leave the same.

The nurse looks down at the illustrator's sketch. She had expected it to be another image of Hansel and Gretel, a series the woman had been working on for some time. It was for this reason, the illustrator said—it must have been weeks ago now—that she had to stop eating. She needed to study, she told the nurse, what it meant to starve. But now, catching the image on her page, the nurse sees that it's not two children in the forest but the comet, set to come tonight. She leans over the illustrator, and briefly scans the courtyard to see if anyone is watching. When she sees that no one is, she closes her eyes and inhales deeply, smelling the illustrator's hair.

Edmond Halley's niece is lying in bed, fearing the threat of becoming a woman and all it entails. Though she is not yet a decade old, she has felt within her a kind of revolt, the sense of impending rupture. Sometimes she has to look at her hands to confirm they are there. Sometimes she has to prompt herself to breathe. She knows these are private ventures, and that her challenges in navigating the space between her body and her mind are all her own, but she also knows that this can only last until she becomes a woman. Then everything will be bared.

The sound of her father's voice downstairs is interrupted by the sound of her uncle's. One of them pounds on the table, and then they both break into a laugh. Inside, she detects a bit of her receding, as though her days on Earth are folding back. She is waiting for her brother's breathing to grow steady, for the pipe of his neck to relax and let the breath through. She holds him, inhales then exhales, so that their bodies are in tandem. She situates him so that he looks out the window, a subtle gesture, the promise of fresh air. Nothing is going to hurt me, she whispers, and he wraps his hand around to squeeze her arm, his breath slowing now, growing even. Nothing is going to hurt me, she tells him, but what he hears is what she does not say: there is nothing to fear.

The nurse looks at the illustrator, then out at the yard full of women. The comet is coming tonight. Given the curve of the orbit and the revolution of the Earth, this will be the closest the comet has ever come. It is said Earth will pass right through the tail. There are rumors that the comet will hit, or that the air will grow poisoned with cyanogen. The nurse watches the illustrator run her palm along the edge of her sketch, framing it in shadow. She doesn't want to reduce the illustrator's story to a tragedy, but it is so sad in her mind that it becomes absurd. Like a fairy tale, she softens the horror so that it can be fully faced.

The illustrator refused to eat for four days before the nurse was told the doctors planned to force-feed her. The nurse hadn't believed them, until they'd said there were suffragettes on hunger strike in Britain, and doctors there had perfected the art. She couldn't bear to be in the room when they did it, had feigned ill, and another nurse had taken her place. She'd felt guilty afterward, and took extra care tending the sores on the illustrator's lips and gums where she was cut from the trauma of putting the tube down her throat. That was the day the illustrator's fast ceased. The next week, the nurse brought her an empty cookie jar and told the illustrator she'd gladly fill it whenever she wanted. The illustrator only wanted gingerbread, and the nurse obliged, folding the cookies in brown paper and planting them in the jar that lived under the illustrator's bed.

Now, the illustrator sketches and the nurse smells her hair, and with her eyes still closed, she barely understands what she is doing when she asks the illustrator: If you knew the end of the world was coming, what would you draw?

Edmond Halley's niece is lying in bed, holding her brother whose breath is even now. She is imagining trajectories for herself: her strangeness is detected and she is sentenced to death by drowning; a terrible something befalls someone close to her and she is accused, then killed by beheading; she cannot have children or her children die in her womb or her children are born and then die, and she is burned at the stake. It is this last possibility that haunts her, because it has happened so often to women her family once knew.

Downstairs, she hears her father and uncle clear the table, listens to her father say goodnight. It feels like the room is fractured and pulling her forward, a kaleidoscope. She gathers the thoughts that haunt the room of her mind and orders them into the shelves she's built there. She asks her brother if he wants to know the story of what unfolds beneath their feet, in the center of the Earth, and he nods, lies back in her arms. She clears her throat and looks out the window as she tells him.

Earlier, her uncle had been outside, preparing for the comet. He spent months calculating its arrival and finally determined the best place from which to see it would be the country, where his sister lives. His niece walked outside to where he'd set up his equipment and asked him about the logic of comets—how they were born and how they behaved and what would become of this one. Her uncle had informed her that comets are chaotic and abstract, moving without much logic at all. But they move with passion, his niece said. That is why they are so fast.

Her uncle looked at her then and asked her to come near. She approached him and he kneeled down in front of her so that their faces were even. What do you think about comets? he asked her, and she looked up at the sky. Tell me a story about comets, he asked her, and she thought for a moment before she said this:

When the world began, there was a single mass of rock. But because of different kinds of force and power, as years went on, the pressure grew and boiled and pushed and bred until one day it broke. And when it broke, the rock dispersed into a million smaller rocks, and every small rock called the others his brothers and sisters. The air, which was then very strong because it was still young, hugged and polished the rocks to make them smooth orbs, and on one of those orbs grew flames—that is the Sun—and on one of those orbs grew people—that is our Earth. The Earth and the Sun are siblings, born from the same family.

But the smallest orb became impatient, and so she left our region of the universe to discover what lies on the limits of the galaxy. She learned a great deal—about who to trust, how to sacrifice, what to believe and why to fear and when to hope. And every time she learned more, she would make the long trek back and return to see her brother, the Sun, for his job was at the center of the universe and he could not leave his post. She would report to him what she had learned. Come with me, she would ask him, to the safe harbors of the edge, where your demand is not so great. Come with me and live on the outskirts where you can Learn and Love and Lose, the three great obligations. And though every time the Sun refuses to go with her, his sister star returns. And though we put trust in the Sun to stay where he belongs, some of us wait for the day that he says yes. Some of us wait for the day he tells his sister I will come, and he abandons us to cold and dark and dread.

Halley looked at his niece then, and she knew what he was thinking. He had told her that the only celestial bodies that follow the path of an orbit are planets, that comets are varied and wild. What she was suggesting was absurd, but she liked the way it sounded. She liked the way it made the strange familiar and the wrong somehow true.

Years from this moment, after Halley has met with and befriended Isaac Newton, after he's traveled by ship around the world, improved the engineering of the diving bell, and explained how solar heating affects monsoons, Edmond Halley will get news that his niece has died. He will think of her and the way she told him the story of the comet's return, as though she'd been composing it in her brain for years. He will not know if it is her narrative or the strange behavior of the comet he observed that night that has kept the evening in his head for all these years. He will think about the way her narrative tried to make order of chaos, not unlike Greek myths or German folktales. He will think about her story and its commitment to circuit, to orbit, to return. He will open a bottle of wine and dig out the notes he crafted that evening; he will measure, debate, and sketch. Then he will clear his desk and begin a letter to Newton.

The nurse asks the illustrator again: What would you draw if you knew the world was ending? And the illustrator hands the nurse her sketch of Halley's Comet and puts her hands on the nurse's face, smiles the saddest smile the nurse has ever seen. The illustrator makes their foreheads touch, and then she kisses her, deeply and with a gentle but frank passion, and the nurse does not pull away. When they are done, the nurse will look around, but all she'll see is other patients, none of whom glance her way. The illustrator will kiss her again, briefly, and then say: I would draw the story of us.

Long after Edmond Halley is dead, though the world thought for years his projection about the return of the Comet of 1682 was a farce, the comet will come back exactly as he had predicted: December 25, 1759. Once a lifetime, he had computed, the comet follows its orbit away from our cosmic system and then back toward it, until it wraps itself around our sun, then leaves again. The day this is confirmed and forever after, the comet will be his. Dead for seventeen years, he will tell no one the strange place from which his theory derived.

Edmond Halley's niece is lying in bed. She has finished the tale about the beings who live beneath Earth's crust. The story devolved a bit toward the end, she thought—her stories are always moving toward the sad and ominous, but usually he is sleeping by the time they are done. This is the case tonight. He is fast asleep, dreaming of everything below, dreaming of the world inside their own.

She slides herself from beneath him and stretches him out, pulls the covers around his form. She stretches out beside him, uncovered, and wills herself to organize her thoughts: the shady thoughts on a shelf in the back, behind a closed and locked door, the safe thoughts at the front. But when she thinks of nice things, they always seem to rot: a bouquet of flowers on a table begins to wilt and decay as the tabletop grows dusty; the sunset on a pond disappears and then the water recedes quickly, until it's an empty abyss. She thinks about the comet up there in the sky and how her uncle told her it would look like a tail of light slowly moving across the night. But all she can imagine is the comet shifting so that it moves toward her, growing ever larger, ever closer, until it hits.

When the nurse arrives at the Asylum for Women the day after Halley's Comet has left, she will be told the illustrator is gone. When she doesn't understand, they will inform her that she escaped and no trace of her had been left. Her breathing will quicken. She will go to the illustrator's room and search for some kind of sign left for her. She will find it underneath the bed, in the corner, covered by old blankets, in the cookie jar.

The nurse will pull out a new series of sketches of Hansel and Gretel. She will flip through the pages and she'll see the whole story: the two siblings abandoned to wander in the woods; the sweet house in the forest; the witch who tries to eat them; the witch shoved in the oven and burned alive. But unlike all the other versions, in this series, the story is illustrated from above, as though the clouds are witnessing the story unfolding below. She'll be haunted by how gothic and surreal the imagery is, how this angle creates an added eeriness. She had never imagined the story of Hansel and Gretel as sublime, but here there is both horror and beauty in the rendering.

Edmond Halley's niece has fallen asleep. The husband of his sister has gone to bed, too. Edmond Halley walks out his sister's front door to get a bit of air. The comet is coming, he thinks. He does not yet know that this celestial body has visited Earth before and it has been recorded. He does not yet know that one day they will call this comet his. At this point in the history of the sky, nothing is named for him.

Behind him, he hears the door open; it is his sister. It should arrive in just an hour, he tells her, and she looks up, pulls her shawl around her shoulders.

When we were young, she tells him, I thought my world revolved around you. And here, I learn it still does.

He stands next to his sister and they look at the sky. His sister tilts her head so that it falls upon his shoulder. The sky, she says. Infinite and enigmatic, he says. And she: A reminder that we cannot meet every story's end. She shivers and he puts his arm around her, pulls her close.

The nurse will take the illustrator's sketches and sell them to a publisher. The sale and subsequent royalties will be sent to the art colony where the illustrator once lived. This is how *The Illustrated Hansel and Gretel* will reach hundreds of thousands of children's shelves. The nurse will retire from her work and place the cookie jar in a box inside her attic. And when, years later, that box is opened, the nurse long deceased, her family will take the jar to a garage sale, the inside full of spiders and their webs.

Edmond Halley's niece is fast asleep, while outside her window Edmond Halley watches the night sky with his sister by his side. It is then the comet breaks open the night. His sister sees the sharp brand across the black vastness, as though someone has split it like a skin, light pouring from the wound. It makes its advance and she thinks of her brother, the man who told her this would come. She thinks it is a kind of magic, the way he can portend. We cannot meet every story's end, Edmond Halley's sister thinks, looking at the smear across the sky. And then, though she tries to put it out of her mind, she thinks about the strangeness of her daughter.

Not until the illustrator is very old and frail, all the women she shared her bed with long dead, will she find a copy of *The Illustrated Hansel and Gretel* at a used bookstore in a city in the north. She will find herself unsteady, and she'll reach for a shelf to hold herself right. In a chair, she'll peel open the cover and flip through the work she once knew intimately, the work that came from her hands. Then she'll think back on the memory of her spell in the asylum. She will think of the nurse and her father, neither of whom she ever again saw. She will think of the comet that portended the end of the world. It is coming back, rounding its course and returning. She will wonder what the comet will see in the future. She will wonder what the comet has witnessed in the past. She will close *The Illustrated Hansel and Gretel* and read on the cover that it was illustrated by Anonymous.

Because its luster is as powerful as dawn, Edmond Halley's niece is wide awake at her window, watching a smudge of fiery rock suspended in the night. What she sees exceeds the limits of the real and she finds her skin grows tight around her form. She listens to her brother's rhythmic rasping as she tries to lock the bad thoughts in the back room of her head, but she feels the comet insisting that she follow. She puts a finger to the window's pane, traces the slow creep. Her sleeping brother wheezes, and she makes her breathing match his as her finger charts the route.

But that is all to come. For now there is only this: a brother and a sister looking at the night sky, the air around them kinetic. This is Caius, France, 1682, and everything is still to come.

| 1378 | 1456 | 1531 | 1605 | 1682 | 1759 | 1835 |
| 1910 | 1986 | 2061 | 2136 | 2211 | 2286 | 2365 |

EPISODES TOWARD AN ELEGY FOR HALLEY'S COMET

1910

Mouths, the illustrator thinks, this story is full of mouths: mouths that cannot be fed, mouths belonging to children that fill themselves with the witch's bait, mouths of ovens that consume, the mouth of the witch who wants to eat the children. We think of this as a story about two children abandoned in a wood by their parents and the way breadcrumbs fail to lead them home. We think of this as a story about escaping supernatural atrocities. But perhaps it is really a story about how to eat, who to fill the gut with, and why. Perhaps this is a story about the way the body aches to be satisfied, and how we call this both hunger and desire.

In the corners of her studio, spiders have dwelled, and in dwelling, left their webs.

1378

Do you know The Way? Hansel asks. And Gretel: Yes. She has learned how to mislead gracefully, convincingly. She knows all about deception and duplicity. Her job is to ease unrest, and inventing fictions is the best method of doing so. Half her work is tricking him into trusting himself and the other half is giving him the tools to make the right decisions. She doesn't know it yet, but she will find that these are the first steps toward being an adult.

1910

Mouths, the illustrator thinks. The hardest task of illustrating is choosing which lines of the prose to put into action. Illustration should amplify the text. Illustration should be a mechanism for helping the story breathe. Or rather, illustration should be the instrument that invites the reader to digest—a break in the forward propulsion of time, the same way silence punctuates music. That is why they call silence a rest.

She has studied the tale intensely. What she didn't know before she took up this project: that the Brothers Grimm are not the story's authors, but its keepers, recorders, and curators. That folktales once lived only in the memory of those who passed the stories through generations and across hills and prairies, so that their telling was an ephemeral event. That the story of Hansel and Gretel has been categorized by a very specific system and that system places it in a family of stories deemed Otherworldly Opponents.

Mouths, the illustrator thinks. Imagine the mouth that invites the body of another. It could be an act that instigates pleasure or it could be an act that inaugurates pain.

1378

What did you dream last night? Gretel asks Hansel. I dreamt that all the flat planes in the sky—the moon, the clouds—had width, like you and me. I dreamt that the sun and moon were spherical like fruit. I dreamt the forest lasted forever and, instead of reaching the end, the world curved and we kept walking until we traversed the whole earth and met the place from where we started.

What did you dream?, Hansel asks Gretel. She looks at him and says she dreamt that she was burned until she became ashes and then he gave the ashes to the wind. In this way, she traveled across great distances, plural and multiplied, seeing everything simultaneously, all places and all times.

She says this, but it is a lie. She cannot come to tell him that she no longer dreams.

1835

Jacob and Wilhelm Grimm are standing outside. They are watching the night sky and thinking about the third edition of their collection of tales. Under Wilhelm's pen, the stories have morphed, moved further from their origins to become more palatable and refined. But something unsettles Wilhelm about the way he's shaping them. He worries that in honing them, the stories are growing toward his desires and wants and not those of the folk. He looks over to his brother, then looks up at the sky. He thinks: Illness, glass enclosures, spider webs. He thinks: Preservation, collaboration, loss. He thinks: Ashes, mazes, mouths. He thinks: Once upon a time.

The comet is coming, he thinks. He steps outside to look up at the stars and what he thinks is: The infinite expanse.

1910

The logic of the breadcrumb. There is something like poetry to the idea; to leave a bit here and there, a set of clues that are only helpful for one who knows to look. A set of clues that would otherwise go unnoticed.

2211

Two space probes disseminate the following into the infinite beyond:
01001000 01100001 01101110 01110011 01100101 01101100
00100000 01100001 01101110 01100100 00100000 01000111
01110010 01100101 01110100 01100101 01101100 00101100
00100000 01100110 01101001 01110010 01110011 01110100
00100000 01100101 01100100 01101001 01110100 01101001
01101111 01101110 00100000 00110001 00111000 00110001
00110010 0001010 0001010

Translated, it reads: "Hansel and Gretel, first edition 1812."

1835

Jacob Grimm looks up to the sky and he can see the comet getting ever closer. Imagine watching us from up there. Imagine all that the comet has seen. It grows close and then rides its orbit around our sun and back to the end of our universe, only to be slung our way again. Does it look like much has changed from up there? We have marked this earth in so many wrong ways, Jacob thinks. Does the comet know? We are born and sleep and earn keep and pay and lie and die. We cut down trees and empty oceans and kill beasts. Does the comet wonder if, on one of these orbits, it will return to find there is nothing left, a vast void where once stood our grand planet? Or will the comet even notice we are gone, our obliteration just another blemish, another body of rock that has failed and faded in the infinite chasm?

2365

Because its inhabitants treat their world poorly, the rules of the universe change. What seems certain in one decade is indefinite in the next. For centuries the comet that comes every seventy-five years was thought to be safe—it was not a threat. In fact, it was said to be dying, falling apart with the great force that fueled its travels, such that it would eventually dissolve. But the Earth is an unstable stone on which its occupants are planted. It must be tended with care, or else it will rebel. Our rock tells us when it's hurt or yearning, and we must listen. Otherwise, one morning we may find it no longer wants to revolve.

When illness invades a body—of flesh and tissue or of melted rock and crumbled shell and glass and bone—suddenly everything is possible. This is the first step in understanding that everything expires.

1378

Hansel and Gretel at a river, quenching their thirst. Gretel asks her brother to look at her. She wets her thumb with her tongue and uses it to wipe a bit of dirt from his forehead and cheek. He watches her work and thinks: Our lives will never again be in such close proximity. It will always be a moving away from each other, from this point on.

Which is to say, to love a sibling is to anchor your life to a series of sanctioned departures.

1910

The illustrator reads the story. Then she reads it again. She thinks about the way mouths operate in the story, how it is all about filling openings. She decides she is not interested in drawing this tale as so many others have, illustrating the world in childhood mirages. The story is real, she thinks as she reads it an eleventh and twelfth time. It is a story about abandoned youth and the stigma that surrounds women, be they stepmothers or witches. It is about the lure of the domestic, the way it tastes sweet. It is about the fear of being eaten but it is also about the fear that eating will satisfy cravings we can only vaguely know.

The illustrator thinks about how the story is fact in the safe costume of fiction. How to illustrate an archaic story that is true and time-less, she thinks. How to illustrate the real.

1378

Gretel holds Hansel's hand as they move through the wood. Dusk is coming on and he is telling her a story. Gretel, he says then, stopping her. Gretel, he says. She has been listening and so she knows he wants to tell her.

From above, the trees cannot hear what Hansel tells her, cannot see Gretel kiss her brother's sweaty bangs and say, her mouth against his forehead, Everything moves in an orbit. She tastes his sweat on her lips. The trees cannot hear her say, You are part of a much bigger tale.

2365

The comet tumbles across the sky, making its approach. It breaks and dissolves and advances, boring a channel through space.

1910

The illustrator considers what it means to be in the forest, in the wood. She considers the characters that populate the narrative. She wants to crawl inside it, to enter the domain of the story she is trying to depict.

She is grateful she is not a writer, for writing is a ghostly, haunted thing. It permits one to enter different temporal dimensions. It allows one to enter different human psyches. It requires one to manipulate the feelings of another until one elicits a particular response.

To read is to consume, to put the book on the tongue and push it down the throat. She reads the story again and again, silently. She catches herself in the glass of the window and for a moment, she does not know the lips that mouth the words.

2211

Two space probes disseminate the following into the infinite beyond:
01001110 01100101 01111000 01110100 00100000 01110100
01101111 00100000 01100001 00100000 01100111 01110010
01100101 01100001 01110100 00100000 01100110 01101111
01110010 01100101 01110011 01110100 00100000 01110100
01101000 01100101 01110010 01100101 00100000 01101100
01101001 01110110 01100101 01100100 00100000 01100001
00100000 01110000 01101111 01101111 01110010 00100000
01110111 01101111 01101111 01100100 01100011 01110101
01110100 01110100 01100101 01110010 00100000 01101000
01101001 01110011 00100000 01110111 01101001 01100110
01100101 00100000 01100001 01101110 01100100 00100000
01101000 01101001 01110011 00100000 01110100 01110111
01101111 00100000 01100011 01101000 01101001 01101100
01100100 01110010 01100101 01101110 00101110

Translated, it reads: "Next to a great forest there lived a poor wood-cutter, his wife, and his two children . . ."

1835

Beginnings, Wilhelm thinks. There is always the issue of beginnings. How to get the thing off the ground, how to initiate, to launch. It has to do with offering a series of possibilities and then deciding on a single route. It has to do with purging the list until there is only one option left. He and his brother have been working with the tales for years now, molding and shaping their form, settling on the best iterations, cutting and pruning and leaving things implied. The question is whether the work they've done is right or wrong. Wilhelm looks up and scans the sky for the comet. He recalls a conversation with Jacob when they first undertook their work. In order to record a tale, something must always be lost. Some things must be left unsaid and disguised. The art of storytelling, his brother said, is all about where and how to leave the voids.

1910

The illustrator studies the spider web in the corner of her studio, the ordered way the spiraling rings are perfectly spaced. She imagines it human-sized. If it were, it would look like a net. It would look like a cage made of rope.

In order to fully understand the story of the two siblings, she had spent some time growing acquainted with hunger. She had tried to know the feeling of being cleanly and completely empty, until each corner of her form ached in unfamiliar ways. Research, in order to understand what it meant to hunger in the body, to fear that hunger in the mind.

Endings. There is always the question of whether or not to let the narrative conclude with text or image. It is a difficult decision, especially when it comes to the work of this story, for the final line conveys that they live happily thereafter. But that is not the end at all, the illustrator thinks. In some ways, that is the beginning. Now they have returned, and they have a history. They have entered the forest and in entering found themselves in the middle of a story about mouths and transgression. The forest, the illustrator thinks, is where children go to grow up.

2211

The probes disseminate: 01010100 01101000 01100101 00100000
01110111 01101111 01101111 01100100 01100011 01110101
01110100 01110100 01100101 01110010 00100000 01110100
01101000 01101111 01110101 01100111 01101000 01110100
00111010 00100000 01001000 01101111 01110111 00100000
01100011 01101111 01110101 01101100 01100100 00100000
01101000 01100101 00100000 01100001 01101110 01100100
00100000 01101000 01101001 01110011 00100000 01110111
01101001 01100110 01100101 00100000 01100110 01100101
01100101 01100100 00100000 01110100 01101000 01100101
01101001 01110010 00100000 01100011 01101000 01101001
01101100 01100100 01110010 01100101 01101110 00100000
01110111 01101000 01100101 01101110 00100000 01110100
01101000 01100101 01111001 00100000 01101000 01100001
01100100 00100000 01101110 01101111 01110100 01101000
01101001 01101110 01100111 00100000 01100110 01101111
01110010 00100000 01110100 01101000 01100101 01101101
01110011 01100101 01101100 01110110 01100101 01110011
00111111 00101110 00100000

Translated, it reads: ". . . The woodcutter thought: How could he
and his wife feed their children when they had nothing for themselves?. . ."

2365

From above, the comet hurls toward Earth at a speed that resists time. It burns and flames and propels through the air. Earth thinks the great comet is dissolving, losing strength every time it visits and then retreats. But the comet behaves in response to the acts that unfold on the rock that once teemed with life. It listens and replies.

1910

In the illustrator's head, the children eat the witch's house. It seems to be about subversion, the illustrator thinks: usually a house eats us, its door swinging like a tongue, our bodies living in its gut. But the image that most haunts the illustrator is that of Gretel crying tears of blood. Gretel, seeping blood, in fear and foul ways. Gretel bleeding from the eyes and mouth. She would be about the age at which the blood runs, the illustrator thinks. Then she thinks: How to depict any of it at all?

The illustrator looks at the giant shells upon her windowsill, the webs that fill its hollows. She thinks about the way her skin is porous, the way canvas feels along her fingertips, the impossible color of the moon. We are a strange and wonderful kind of creature, she thinks, always wanting to look.

1378

It is getting dark and they can hear the sounds the forest makes. Gretel holds her brother from behind, her arm a brace across his middle. She can feel her brother's beating heart. Did you remember to wear your invisible cloak? she asks. And he says, Yes. I have it on now. That's good, Gretel tells him. With it on, no one will see you.

They lie on a bed of soft leaves she has collected and they hold each other close. She can feel his heart slowing a bit, though she can also smell his sweat. When the world ends, it will end because of heat, Gretel says. This is a story she has told him time and time again, a story they tell each other. When the world ends, it will end because of heat, Hansel repeats. There will be a great storm with thunder and lightning but no rain. And Gretel: The lightning will strike, and it will be breathtaking. But we won't turn to ash, nor to fire. Why not? she asks her brother. And her brother replies, as he has replied innumerable times before: We will bury ourselves in sand, and when the lightning hits, we'll turn to glass.

1910

In the windows of her studio, the illustrator sees that the fog is settling and for a moment she can't remember if it is morning or night. She threads her fingers around her charcoal pencil, the one with the soft tip, best for rendering shadow. She has been in this room for hours, thinking about feeding, consumption, the art of filling the mouth in order to fill the gut. She has been in this room for hours thinking about the way the promise of something sweet on the tongue is the oldest sort of seduction.

The illustrator hears someone knock and then open the door. It's time, she is told, and she rises from her seat. She feels comfortable leaving her room because she has a plan, an idea of how she will render the story this time. It will all be viewed from above, as if an ethereal lens lingers in the top of the trees, witnessing the tale. It will feature the intricate design of the woods, the labyrinth leading the siblings from their safe home to the center of the maze, wherein the woman's house lies. She will work all night depicting the story in this way, throw out her older versions. Beginnings, the illustrator thinks, and nods to the spider web.

She walks outside and the fog has fully vanished. She stands and watches the great comet move like a lazy yawn through the sky.

We put ourselves in prisons, the illustrator thinks. She looks across the way at the sign that says Asylum for Women. Then she scans the crowd for her lover's face, and it is there. They are two women, looking across a vast field, and then they are two women looking up. A growing collection of other women stand together in the field of the asylum and gaze at the comet that passes every seventy-five years. They think: One day. They think: There will come a time.

Which is to say, when enough people have been hurt by coded forms of hate, they will gather and they will start a war.

2211

The probes disseminate: 01001000 01100001 01101110 01110011
01100101 01101100 00100000 01100011 01110010 01110101
01101101 01100010 01101100 01100101 01100100 00100000
01100001 01101100 01101100 00100000 01101111 01100110
00100000 01101000 01101001 01110011 00100000 01100010
01110010 01100101 01100001 01100100 00100000 01100001
01101110 01100100 00100000 01100100 01110010 01101111
01110000 01110000 01100101 01100100 00100000 01110100
01101000 01100101 00100000 01100011 01110010 01110101
01101101 01100010 01110011 00100000 01101111 01101110
01110100 01101111 00100000 01110100 01101000 01100101
00100000 01110000 01100001 01110100 01101000

Translated, it reads: ". . . Hansel crumbled all of his bread and
dropped the crumbs onto the path . . ."

1835

The brothers' eyes are cast toward the sky, watching the comet's tail.
The ending, Wilhelm thinks. The beginning, Jacob thinks.

1378

The center, Gretel thinks, and squeezes her brother's hand.

2365

The comet hurls toward Earth, tumbles chaotically through the infinite region we know as beyond until it undoes everything we have come to know. From afar, the collision looks like a bright freckle on the skin of the cosmos that swells for a moment, then goes out.

1378

Hansel and Gretel are nearing the house. Hansel points to the comet overhead. Is this the end? he asks. His sister takes his hand. They cannot know that over the next hill is the woman and her house of sweets. In the corners of the room they will sleep in tonight, a spider weaves her web. Gretel looks at the way the skin on her hands is cracked and the nails are caked with dirt. Is she a child or is she a woman?

I can't know, Gretel says. She brushes her brother's hair back into its part, runs her tongue along her top lip. I can't know, she says, but it will be the wrong end if it is.

1378　　1456　　1531　　1605　　1682　　1759　　**1835**

1910　**1986**　**2061**　　2136　　**2211**　　2286　　**2365**

THE MARVELOUS SPIRAL

A VAST VACUUM OF nothing and then a bright menagerie of life. Stars and horizons. The concept of night. The universe begins its memory the moment it breaks open because space curves. This is why force. This is why time.

A bit of star breaks from a larger body and gravity polishes it a track that runs from the center of the galaxy to the end. It clicks into place and becomes compelled to follow this trajectory for a series of endless revolutions.

Meanwhile, on one of the newly formed planets, cells develop, then plants. There is sex and then organs and wings and tails and shells. A nautilus grows and lives and then dies, its body caught in rock and buried. The shell dissipates over the years until all that is left is the echo of its coil.

Sex changes and then there is hair. Then people. Bodies on the ground, shifting.

Self-consciousness. Desire and disgust. The revelation that humans are uniquely equipped to assemble information. The revelation that humans are uniquely equipped to disseminate it.

Languages begin, ripen, slim down, and dissolve. Languages bud in the most remote folds of the earth.

Somewhere someone says: Creation, famine, flood.

Someone else says: Disease.

In the sky, the comet endures its rounds, moves toward and then away from the Sun, its center a vortex of fire and ice that boils and rages. It wants to escape, but invisible laws enforce its sentence, and so it circles without end.

On Earth, adults hold children's hands—when yoked together in a crowd, while facing a threat, with necks bent back, watching the comet above.

Brothers and sisters are born. The formula for siblings is the same—semen from the same man enters the same woman. The distinction is genetic time. Same orbit, different lap.

There is war and want. There is horror and hate. There is love and longing. There are stories.

Cain and Abel. Cassandra and Helenus. Frey and Freyja. Rama and Lakshmana. Hoori and Hoderi. Mawu and Lisa. Hahgwehdiyu and Hahgwehdaetgah. Nut and Geb.

Hansel and Gretel. The story is first told by tongues now long gone. It echoes through the countryside, travels great distances and across the ages. Families install it into the brains of their children and those children grow to become adults. The story is mapped into the mind like a digital blueprint. The brain computes that the story is about strife, abandonment, the possibilities of leaving bits of yourself behind in order to find your way home. Home is used here figuratively, meaning that which is familiar and comfortable and safe.

Somewhere, someone says: Forgive me.

Elsewhere, someone says: Stop.

A spider weaves her web to catch her prey. There is a logic to the way the silk grid is roped to make her home; it follows a mathematical rule that will be known as the marvelous spiral. When she lays a sac of her eggs and that sac breaks open, hundreds of siblings are released to disperse across the world by string or wind or larger creature. The beasts that once called the same pod home never return again.

Two middle-aged sisters. One wants children and cannot have them, so the other offers her womb. A child grows inside and is born and the sisters never tell their daughter in which body she was harvested.

Two young brothers. One needs a kidney and so the other goes under and his is cut out. Neither survive and their father weeps, his hands raised to the night sky.

In an abandoned field, two siblings are digging. They are digging because children are interested in the art of discovery. They are digging in the ground and the sun is growing high and they are sweating.

They are laughing and sweating and one sibling puts a bottle of water to her lips and it is cold and soothes her swollen throat, and how she wants to finish the water in it. But she doesn't. She hands the bottle to her brother.

Someone says: Thank you.

Someone else says: Never mind.

Two brothers hear the stories that orbit the countryside, decide to write them down. One of the stories is that of the siblings whose parents abandon them in the wood, and at night, over drinks, they decide this story is particularly cruel. Through the years they revise the story, carefully editing out that which they cannot face. Before their final edition is published, the story looks almost nothing like it once did. They do not discuss this. They lock hands together in understanding. Then they walk outside to witness the great traveling star move through the sky.

The comet hurls toward Earth but passes it by. Its orbit curves around the Sun, its brother from before the void. The comet mourns, missing its sibling. Every time it makes its return, when it approaches the Sun, a bit of its cosmic flesh is dissolved.

Flowers bloom and rot, snow falls and melts, beasts cover the land, get slain, go extinct. Human bodies emerge from other human bodies, grow tall and walk far, shorten and slow, then lie and fail to rise.

Someone asks: How?

Someone else asks: Why?

Because the brothers wrote it down, the story of Hansel and Gretel continues to morph and evolve. It becomes an opera. It becomes a play. In some versions, there is a duck that takes them home to their father. In some versions, they return home only to learn that they have been transformed into adults.

A woman decides to take a new approach, illustrates the two siblings from above. The aerial view of the narrative strikes those who see the drawings as eerie and unnerving. When the woman disappears, someone takes her drawings to a publisher and the sketches are purchased at an inexpensive price.

A typical print run for a picture book is approved, and 15,000 copies of *The Illustrated Hansel and Gretel* are made. They are disseminated across the world. Older bodies hold younger bodies and place before their eyes the open volume. The imagery haunts everyone in a similar vein, like a song in minor.

From above, the comet makes its pass, swings around the green and blue sphere. But as it curves to see the dark part of the planet, it is surprised to observe something new. After countless laps for an unknown set of eras, now the comet sees no part stays dark when it turns away from the Sun. Instead, thick deposits of light freckle the sphere's skin. What strange forms breed there to make the dark parts flicker?

Below, ships sail across the water, and shortly thereafter, planes sail across the sky. Brothers unite with other brothers. Sisters betray each other. There is ugliness and horror and afterward, there are toasts at meals and braided hair. Hands are held in unity; heads are held in grief. There is blood on cement, and then years pass and a man points to the spot and asks what happened there, and his twin says, I don't see anything.

In an abandoned field, two siblings are digging. They are digging with small metal shovels. One sibling develops a blister, and because the other knows that the best remedy is limiting friction, she lets her brother stop. They do not know that they will grow tall and wise and their roles as siblings to each other will be superseded by their roles in the world: she will be a scholar and he a dancer. Right now, they are not looking forward toward the future, but down. The brother watches his sister with admiration, and when her shovel's thrust makes an unfamiliar sound, they look at each other as if to say, everything's been moving toward right now.

The echo of the nautilus's coil is stamped into rock and buried for a thousand years. It is dark and protected underground, until the day the brother and sister release it. They do not know that one day she will study the ways stories persist when they are not written down. They do not know that one day audiences will be held breathless by the way he moves. What they know is that they have found what remains of what was once a nautilus, its imprint left in this rock. They pluck it from the earth and they go home, share a bowl of ice cream, take turns feeling the empty space where the creature once dwelled.

There are 12,212 copies of *The Illustrated Hansel and Gretel*. Some are burned in house fires. Some are drowned in baths. Some are torn apart by small hands and put into garbage bags to be put into a landfill in the earth. Inside 2,371, inscriptions are made; 957 of those inscriptions are to siblings.

After reading her the book, a brother tells his sister that the narrator of a tale lingers vestigial like an abandoned character, peripheral but present, a ghost or spirit lurking along the frame. This is how all narration is an act of speaking through another's mouth.

Another brother tells his sister he never wants to see her again.

Someone says: Be careful.

Another: Don't worry.

The comet approaches, and this time it notices the green has been replaced with brown and grey. It wonders if the orb is sick. When the comet sees the globe get dark, it also sees the light has concentrated, gotten thicker and more dense.

The nautilus shell follows the sister and brother through the years, sharing space on each of their dressers. It listens as the sister tells her brother different versions of the same tales from around the world. It watches as the brother models for his sister thirteen perfect fouette turns.

There are 7,929 copies of *The Illustrated Hansel and Gretel*. Some are purchased new at stores. Some are passed down and the price is haggled at sales in people's yards. One copy, torn and tattered and with a broken spine, is handed to a middle-aged woman as her inheritance. When she opens the cover and sees the forty-year-old outline of her hand next to her dead sister's, she sobs.

Seasons turn and years pass and bodies are burned and buried. Mysteries are solved or forgotten. Problems find solutions.

Someone says: Hurry.

Someone else says: Wait.

When she goes to college, the brother tucks the nautilus shell into his sister's bag. Months later she sends it to him for his birthday, along with a catalog of other prehistoric remains. A year later, he sends it to her in the mail inside a ceramic box he's had custom made to fit its shape. She gives it back to him before she leaves for graduate school, their initials professionally etched into the back.

A girl dies too young and her brother pounds on her headstone with his fists until his hands are bloody. He finishes school, marries, divorces, learns he cannot bear children, works a lifetime at a job at which he does not thrive. He turns thirty, then fifty, then seventy. All this time he is haunted by the sister he lost. One day he is eighty and he returns to her grave, which he learns is covered in crawling ivy, her name illegible because the empty valleys of each letter sketched in the rock are full of soil and mold. When he arrives, the day has just broken open, the sun turning the frost on the grass to dew. He cannot read the headstone, and this is how he knows that life is cruel. He turns around to sit on the patch of grass below which his sister lies and leans his back against the stone that, under the mire of time, bears their shared name.

He imagines the years reversing, so that the sand in the hourglass is vacuumed up rather than falling down. He reverses the years until he is back in the moment when all of this began, their uncle reading to them from a picture book.

There are 5,094 copies of *The Illustrated Hansel and Gretel*. There are 4,094 copies of *The Illustrated Hansel and Gretel*. There are 3,094 copies of *The Illustrated Hansel and Gretel*.

The comet bores a channel through the nameless elsewhere, and though it cannot see what unfolds below, there is a new sensation loitering along the borders of the orb: the fine mist of something more.

Someone says: Next time.

Someone else says: Help.

Bodies grow ill and then mend, or grow ill and share that illness with others. People care for their sick and mourn them before they are gone. Siblings sacrifice for each other, unite and leave their families behind. Siblings maintain the memory of their dead by holding hands and telling stories, giving voice to those now gone.

Meanwhile, a brother tells a sister all his good stories, exhausts her through the evenings as he grows increasingly ill. She listens and laughs, then weeps, and they hold hands. He gives her the nautilus for the last time. And it is only then, only now that he is at the edge, that she realizes she has not recorded his stories, on paper or through sound. She, the folktale scholar. It is only when he's at the edge that she realizes all his stories live only in her memory now.

She says: Not yet.

The woman says: Not yet.

In the dark of the night, in a field, on her knees, a sister says: Not yet.

Someone gets the idea to create a multimodal catalog of our information. Suddenly everyone is connected. Our stories get shared more easily but also authorship gets complicated. Because space is infinite here, people have to fight over something else. They decide it will be time.

Someone says: Things are getting better.

Someone else says: Things could be worse.

The story of Hansel and Gretel continues to evolve. In some versions, the siblings are sent into space to fight an alien witch. In some versions, the siblings are a computer virus caught by the breadcrumbs they leave. People write articles and then books about how pliable the story is and how this is the reason it has managed to persist.

A spider weaves her web to catch her prey. She lays a sac of her eggs and it breaks open. This is the same way she was born and survived, found the place she now calls home. This is how her children will, too.

There are 1,485 copies of *The Illustrated Hansel and Gretel*. People pass stories on to be remembered. People pass stories on to forget. The world seems to get smaller and larger, at once.

In an abandoned field, one sibling is digging. She is thinking of how few years her brother walked this earth, how his body installed fear and beauty on the stage and possibility on the street, how that body is now reduced to bits of bone and powder. She has placed the ashes of her brother's form into a cookie jar and now she puts the jar into the ground. She is weeping and wiping the discharge of her sorrow with her sleeve. When she has covered the cookie jar with soil, she places the nautilus on top, then curls her body on Earth's crust above her brother. She does not look up at the night sky to see the comet passing.

Two space probes are released into the beyond. They move through the decades, orbiting planets and gathering data, then moving further until they exit our universe. They are twin machines that contain a record of this world, information that can be decoded so that others might understand it. They pass the comet only once, and each regards the other with respect.

There are 482 copies of *The Illustrated Hansel and Gretel* when the earth revolts. First it is rain that lasts for months, storms so well-fueled they create an ongoing core of eddying water that never tires. Then, because the earth is warm and soft from heat and rain, there are eruptions and quakes that break the land, give it new dimensions. The lightning from the storms sparks fires that cannot be put out. There are mudslides and erosion. There are years of heat that make the oceans bigger and the continents small. Insects that could not live through winters now reproduce in droves, and with them comes disease. Everything becomes a vast and reframed landscape, new and wild. Life becomes delicate and raw. Communities form but struggle. They seek to harness their archive of knowledge, but it lives as invisible encryptions somewhere among the stars. Analog hardware cannot access the virtual world, and so it stays trapped in the ether, nearby but also remote.

Someone says: Hurry.

Someone else says: Please.

One night a young woman gets lost coming back from the river. She is her community's water carrier, and while she's made this trip before, this time the clouds veil the stars that show her the way home. It is then she comes upon a house that is halfway intact. It looks like a rare treat in the middle of a desert, meant for only her. It takes her time to understand how to ascend the stairs, but her desire to see what lies at the top compels her. When she arrives, having climbed with hands and knees, she sees a wall has been broken open, and she looks upon the vista where to the north there is a grid of fires in her community's unique pattern, and she knows how to get home. When she turns around, ready to start her journey, she sees a shelf on which live a very evenly stacked collection of thin codexes. She pulls one from the shelf, and when she opens it, she learns she cannot read the words. It looks to be the lost language, which long ago died out.

She sits on the floor of what was once a child's room and she finds— for the first time in her life—her belief becomes suspended. For while she does not understand the line of symbols, the images seem to her both haunting and familiar, like déjà vu. It is the story of two siblings, but told from above, so that when she is looking down at the page she is also looking down through the canopy of the woods. She is not viewing sutured sheets of paper, but has entered in mind and body the forest on the page.

There are 31 copies of *The Illustrated Hansel and Gretel* and no one reads the words.

A clock unmanned for a century chimes. A natural fire begins and then goes out. A nautilus fossil inscribed with two siblings' initials sits idle in a field.

Because it makes contact with other celestial bodies and those bodies shift its balance with the Sun, the comet's orbit morphs. It grows closer to the planet. One day, it fears that it may hit. As it is riding its orbit, the comet watches the Earth grow ever larger until it sees what crawls on the surface, which is, it learns, nothing. The planet contains the dregs of what was once human life, now covered in green.

Trees grow in the center of bed frames. Moss covers bridges and bushes bust through asphalt roads. Ivy crawls up the side of skyscrapers in empty cities. Plants nest where humans once did—in the rooms of houses with collapsed roofs, in the seats of subway trains and restaurants. Mushrooms in a range of colors grow from open books. Ferns emerge from the frames of broken windows.

The discharge of our kind has been reanimated by the natural world so that the things we once found important become ruins beneath a much stronger force. It cannot be known how many times the tale has been told, but it is told no more, at least on this abandoned sphere. And now the comet comes to know its own finale as it races toward the polished rock it's watched for years. As it approaches, it thinks perhaps it has been destined for this end since the moment it broke from its brother at the center of the system. It has finally been released from its orbit, abandoned by the laws of the sky. Its approach is imminent now, and it watches as its force starts to bore a fiery crater on the rock's skin. There are four copies of *The Illustrated Hansel and Gretel* and then, in an instant, there are none.

Long before all this, centuries before, in an abandoned field, two siblings are running. They are running and trying to catch each other when they see a nautilus shell. The younger picks it up and flips it over, reads the initials carved into the back. He starts to dig, his sister's body just a point on the horizon. He is hoping to find what lies below before she stops him. Her form grows larger as she approaches, and he is digging with his hands, soil firmly fitting underneath his fingernails. He feels the smooth outside of a container, just as his sister draws close. He sees her head and then the way the wind blows her hair, then the wrinkles in her forehead. From the ground, he pulls out the treasure: a cookie jar. He is running on adrenaline fueled by his innate sense that magic is still possible. But his sister sees what her brother pulls from the earth and she knows. He hands it to her and she turns away from him and crouches down, lifts the lid and tips the jar to get a better look. The ash is not thin; it is riddled with charred bone. She wants to believe it is a pet, but her body is too advanced to wish.

Just then a great sound cuts through the sky. The siblings look up and they know that this is it, the tailed star that was portended. This must surely be the closest it has ever been. It is breathtaking, eerie, a reminder that their bodies, like their troubles, are trivial.

Glass lasts a million years, the sister says, and he holds up the nautilus fossil. She takes it, runs her fingers over the impressions. She puts it inside the jar, then tucks it snugly into the ground and covers it back up with soil. Some stories should not be rewritten.

No one says: Every tale that lasts is real, even if it's not true.

No one says: Once upon a time.

No one says anything in this region of the universe, but in the dark parts of the infinite unknown, the twin machines that hold the human record approach Earth's sister world. And on the surface of that sphere, one sibling whispers to another: every end is really a beginning.

1378   1456   1531   1605   1682   1759   1835

1910   **1986**   2061   2136   2211   2286   2365

GRETEL AND THE WITCH

WHEN I AM YOUNG and don't know much about the way lives curl and coil around each other and that we call this love, I ask my brother why he does not want the lips of girls. We are playing in the sandbox, that liminal space where other worlds are encouraged to open. He looks at me and I cannot break the stare. Our castles in the wet sand fall apart.

Years later, we find ourselves on our parents' doorstep. My brother has not wanted the lips of girls for some time, has instead known the mouths of men. Now my brother is ill. There is a correlation, and our parents listen as we disclose this information. We are standing on the porch and I am wondering when our mother will let us into the home in which we were born and raised. I can see through the channel of the house to the back, where the sandbox still lives. It is empty like the top of an hourglass when the time is up.

As we stand there on the porch where we shared popsicles and chalked stick people, where we wiped the dirt from each other's feet before entering the house, our parents don't seem to understand. We try to explain in soft terms: love, men, risk. I am thinking they are not listening, but soon I see my mother hug her heavy middle. I see the skin on her face turn a kind of pale green. She is standing in front of my father, and when he tries to speak she holds up the back of her hand to his chest and he stops. He says her name, and she moves backward, pushes him into the house. He says her name again, over, her name, and my mother is shutting the door very slowly. There is our family on the porch and then there is just my brother and I, the closed door a lesson in how to be alone.

What we do not know is that this scene has been unfolding across the country. I try to imagine the parents in bed at night, in that space before sleep when the mind follows its own set of rules. Do they think of the boys they once greeted with side hugs and half smiles? Do they think of the bangs they once pushed from foreheads, the chins they once held in their palms? Or are they able to revise the past, erase the child from their history as if he never was?

My brother and I walk away from that house, the home in which we were raised. And like two characters in a story, when we step off that porch the rest of the yard shifts into the set of a production; I watch the world around us shift from the familiar site of our childhood yard into a dark and indefinite wood. We are no longer adults, but children who must use all our cunning and savvy to get to the center of the labyrinth, compelled by we know not what.

It should be said that I study folktales. I study folktales because I am interested in what is lost when stories passed on by voice are committed to paper. I study folktales because I am interested in sacrifice.

Once upon a time a brother and a sister were sent to the woods by their parents. It was implied they would not return. The parents could not know that the siblings would meet a witch, nor that they would enlist her in their efforts to survive.

Once upon a time there was a witch who collected chipped cookie jars. She found them here and there and did not know why she felt obliged to keep them. But then again, she thought, pulling the bedcover around the neck of her daughter and tucking it tightly under her chin, what compels us to collect at all? It must have to do with preparation, she thinks. It must have to do with the future and chance.

Once upon a time, I came to the witch for help. I said, My brother is gravely ill and my parents have turned us away, sent us to The Woods. I said, We were taught not to speak to strangers, especially witches, but my brother—, I said. And the witch took us into her house and put us up. And when I eyed the chipped cookie jars lining the shelves on the walls of her kitchen, she saw me. She was carrying my brother upstairs, for his weight had diminished so that he was light as a bag. She saw me eyeing the cookie jars and she said: Help yourself.

All that feels like years ago now. Today marks the beginning of my journey alone.

After the witch tucks in her daughter, she comes into the kitchen, where I am making us tea. It has been a long day. We have buried my brother. I watched my brother grow up and grow out of our small town. I watched my brother grow into the city, and then I watched him grow ill.

The witch sits down, and I see her stir honey in her tea so carefully that the spoon never hits the cup. Soon I hear the soft snores of her daughter. Time feels like it is pleating, so that before and after seem somehow simultaneously now.

I study folktales because I am interested in vanished voices, but I also study folktales because I wonder about The Woods. Behind the sandbox of our youth lies a wide and gaping expanse of trees. When I was young I wanted desperately to enter that domain, to trek the forest in order to learn about the secrets the trees kept. One day, when we were adults and very drunk, I disclosed this to my brother. He laughed long and hard and kicked the air. He was a dancer and his body was this strange and wonderful machine that elegantly navigated the pod of air around it, so that he seemed forever suspended on strings. You realize that sounds like sexual repression? he said. Years of waiting at the entrance to the woods? I gave him a punch on the arm and he feigned hurt. Between us lay the nautilus fossil we had once found in a field, a token of our union. If you really wanted to satiate your curiosity about the unknown, he told me, picking up the fossil, rubbing the hollow with his thumb, you should have followed me into the city.

I want to tell this story the right way, the way in which all the characters are depicted as powerful agents of change, in which they are not victims or heroes, but sensibly composed and well-balanced people. I want to tell this story right, but know this: I study stories, I do not narrate them.

This is why I'm asking for your pardon before I get started. I only have the stories I've read as a guide for how to tell this one. This is why we'll start in the center of the maze. The first question the beast inside the labyrinth asks is, "Why are you here?"

I ask myself this as I am lying on the couch of the witch's house the first night my brother spends under the ground. I pull the covers tight and think: My brother is gone, which means I've made it to the middle. Now the question is: How do I get out?

...

Before the cookie jars were chipped, they lived in a myriad of other houses across the Deep South. They were collected by the witch and her daughter from yard sales.

Before the witch was a witch, she was just a woman.

Once upon a time, the woman had inherited a cemetery with 262 empty plots in a tiny town in The Natural State. She would take her daughter to the cemetery on Sunday afternoons and treat it like a park, playing in the grass. What on earth, the woman thought to herself, am I to do with a cemetery? She pushed the wet bangs from her daughter's sweaty forehead and kissed the tip of her nose.

The cemetery lay near her home, growing lonely. Beneath the surface, the earth was wanting. Beneath the surface, the soil desired.

One day, the woman went to visit a friend at the hospital. The friend was ill and was placed in a corridor with others who were sick. The woman roamed the halls while her friend slept. She noticed a door covered in a red tarp that said CAUTION. The women had read her own fairy tales when she was young and knew to keep away, but something at the core of her being compelled her. It could have derived from the way that red signifies warning but also passion, the way that red is a signal to go away and also to approach. Or perhaps this is part of the plight of women, to be always drawn to a variety of different forms of hurt.

The woman entered the room and in it found a solitary soul, delirious with illness but aware enough to know that he was coming down to this last hours. He was thin as paper, a husk. He asked for his mother, and the woman said she would do what she could do. She did not say there was a chance she could do nothing.

The woman approached The Keepers of Health and asked them why the man had not been cared for, and if his mother was on her way. The Keepers of Health told her he had The Plague that afflicted men who loved men, and so he should not be handled. Even his mother, whom they had contacted, wanted nothing to do with him.

The woman went back into the red room, ready to tell the Man of Paper that his family was not coming. But when she entered that door, the man's face lit up and he called her his mother and took her hand. She stayed with him until the day ended, until the sun fell beneath the horizon and the man made his last blink, then opened his eyes for good. She gently closed them and promised she would take care of the sack of skin he'd left behind.

The Keepers of Health were happy to release the body to the woman. She went from one funeral home to another trying to get the body prepared for burial, but no one wanted it. Eventually she found a crematorium that would conduct the necessary task.

When she got the ashes back, she called the man's mother. The mother hung up on her once, then again. The woman called a third time and as soon as the phone was picked up, she said: If you hang up on me again, I will make sure the obituary lists his cause of death. This is how the woman got the mother to stay on the line. But all the mother said was that her son had been dead to her for years, and his ashes were now the woman's problem.

The woman hung up the phone and looked for something to bury the man in. She looked around the house and found nothing, found instead herself exhausted, squeezed clean of understanding, deeply and irrevocably pained. She found herself weeping on the floor of her kitchen, sobbing with a kind of abandon she had never known. She wept until her face was so swollen her eyes stayed closed. She sat on that floor in her delirium for what length of time she did not know. Her episode must have woken her daughter, for suddenly she heard her child asking her what was wrong.

The woman wiped her face with her sleeve. The woman was cautious. She said she needed a sturdy container that was once loved for a very long-term and important task. Her daughter nodded quickly, as if she understood completely the chore at hand. She left, and a moment later she returned with one of the chipped cookie jars. Here, the daughter said, and the woman took the jar and blew her nose and kissed her child.

Labyrinths incite fear because they are not by design linear. People are afraid of experiences that are not linear, experiences that deviate, diverge, digress. This is because people crave a single course. People want to move up and forward. People want a route that is straight.

The men arrived like water, a stream running from The Big Apple to The Little Rock. She cared for them each, emptied the rooms of her home and gave them beds. The men came and they brought with them their medications and their stories and their art. The walls of the woman's house became populated with beautiful, haunting paintings and her tables adorned with sculptures. The men left her the pages of their manuscripts and the costumes from their performances. Her house became a place of great beauty, though it was also a place of great frustration and pain.

And when she could confirm the men were sleeping, the woman would call their families. She called over and over and the phones would ring and ring. When someone would answer, they would tell her she was a witch. She was a witch with a very dark soul to have taken in men as wrong as their sons. She was a witch for surrounding herself with a group of bodies who had invited The Plague inside themselves. She was a witch for intervening, for the men deserved just what they got. And the witch said: We are speaking of your son. The witch said to the fathers and cousins and grandparents: We are speaking of the child you once cared for and loved, the person with a place at your dinner table and a branch on your family tree. The witch said to the mothers: We are speaking of the child who spent nine months inside you once upon a time.

But the families would not hear. They hung up on her and she was left alone: a dial tone in her ear, a daughter in her bed, a stack of bills growing on her table.

It should be said that she got help long before me. She sought help from the local color, the kind you can only find in the South. To her rescue came the drag queens who put on balls to raise money to care for the dying men. They called her The Witch, but unlike the families she telephoned at night, they said it with a wink. And so she embraced the title and reclaimed the word. For both she and the queens knew the history of women, that too many have been killed because a man told a very elegant fiction and found enough people to believe it.

The ill came and then the ill ceased, and left behind their remains. The witch had the bodies made into ashes. She put the ashes in the cookie jars and then she put the cookie jars in the ground. The earth accepted the jars and held tight around them. The earth asked the sky if the men could rest now and the sky replied by showing the earth its band of clustered stars. Though the woman could not hear the earth speak to the sky, she saw the universe above her. She thought about the men who were beginning to fill her plots and she thought about the disease that riddled their bodies.

Is the disease up there? her daughter asked when she saw her mother staring at the sky. This after they had buried another jar full of ashes, then said several gentle words about the man the jar contained. The woman said she did not know. The woman said she could not know if the sky was free from the illness or if the stars, too, were infected. But if they are, the woman said, let us hope very much that the celestial families invite their children home. Let us hope that the universe beyond our earth is kinder.

Once upon a time, for a group of men who loved men at the end of the worst century, the witch gave them care, affection, and a place to rest.

And the men lay quietly ever after.

. . .

Somewhere right now, people in a factory are making cookie jars. The glass is being set and the lids are being cut and the word COOK-

IE is being carefully impressed from the inside out, so that if a child ran her hand across the jar, she could feel the letters rising to meet her fingers. My fear is that we will need the cookie jars for several years to come.

I wanted to stay. I wanted to help the men who belonged to the same community as my brother: men who love men from the cities, who are artists and have been turned away by their families. Let me be clear: The witch did not ask me to stay—I insisted.

When I move around the house, the men tell me their stories: of the bathhouses that permitted them a freedom known only to their generation, of the theatres they frequented and the bars they called home. The parties, the art, the dancing, the drugs. Then, the rumors. Then, the friends falling first slowly, so there was time to mourn and debate and commune, and then quickly, so that they found themselves empty of tears. They kept their homes stocked with sympathy cards. They kept the flowers from one funeral to reuse at the next. They tell me of those who leave the cities, those who have adopted celibacy. The bathhouses are closed, the theatres empty, a community and culture vanishing. They tell me of those who still linger, wanting, grown thick with health; they gain weight as if to display the proof that some bodies are not ill.

I hear of the men who are gone, and sometimes the women—I hear of the art that litters the streets because the apartments are being emptied and no one is left to take the dead's things. I hear of the men who have been partnered for ten, twenty years—how when one falls to the illness, the other is left homeless because there is no protection for unwed pairs.

I hear of the gentle ways they take care of each other: feeding, wiping, washing. Making meals and changing sheets and tending sores. And staying sane while the mind of their lover swells and then shrinks.

And then, as quick as ice turns to water, they do it again. Another lover, a colleague, a friend. Another lover, a partner, a neighbor, another lover. A stranger. Another lover.

The witch and I tend to the dying men in the rooms of her saccharine house. She pulls the blankets around their necks, wipes their brows, and distributes their medication while the smell of cookies baking wafts through the halls. One day, after telling me his story, a man asks me to tell him one of my own. He is a sculptor, and he was well so recently there is still clay caked under his nails. I tell him that I don't know many stories other than fairy tales, but he is happy to hear one. So, I begin.

Once upon a time, there was this and now, and I am ashamed to say: I don't know how to tell this story.

One evening the phone rings and I answer. Hello? I ask, but there is nothing on the line, just a kind of stuttered breathing. Hello? I say more gently. If this were someone aiming to say rash and horrid things, the person would have said them. Who is there? I ask the mouth on the other end, but it won't speak and so we sit there because I know. I know it is a mother or a father or a grandparent, a brother or a cousin or an aunt. I know it is someone conflicted. What is his name? I ask and the breathing grows less even, as though the person is facing a great encounter. What is his name? I ask again, and the line goes dead.

...

Kinds of cookies the jars contained before they contained the men: pecan, chocolate chip, macadamia nut, peanut butter, custard cream, almond, sugar, gingerbread.

I am doing laundry, cleaning the sheets to rid them of blood and sweat and feces, when the witch's daughter tugs on my shirt. What does the disease look like? the daughter asks. She wants to draw it, then burn it up and put it in a jar so that it, too, might die and the men might be rid of it. It is invisible, I tell her. This is what makes it so dangerous. She takes a new sheet of paper and leaves it blank. Then she asks me to turn it to ashes.

Some nights, after the men are asleep and the witch has put her daughter to bed, after she and I have our tea and she retires herself, I walk the plots and look up at the sky. I put flowers on the graves and I imagine the sky looking down at our sad circumstance. To the sky, we must demand as much attention as a grain of sand. To the sky, we are just another natural phenomenon that will leave an insubstantial trace, a fossilized arrangement of bone here, the crater of a long-melted glacier there. If only we were privileged with such distance, perhaps we could see how minor we all are, all our art and thought and illness and meaning reduced to a bit of debris, the detritus on one of a million spheres stupidly looping nothing.

The phone rings and I answer. Hello? I say, and there is the stutter breathing again. I try to take my form and put it into this invisible figure; I try to put my body in the body of the mouth that breathes on the end of this line. I try to transport myself through the line of the phone to the elsewhere this person occupies and I try to make them me. But when I try to be the body that they are, I fail. It is not for lack of want. I simply cannot come to know the world the way they do. The line goes dead.

The first rule of folklore is that stories cannot be owned. This is what I'm thinking as I watch the bodies around me fall and we do the dirty work of burning them, as I see the forms thin in the beds, the skin marked with lesions, the sheets filthy from waste, the minds going swimmy. I wonder who will tell this story. I look at the bodies surrounding me, a human wasteland, and I wonder who will tell this tale. Who, and also: How?

I think of this at night when I lie in my bed. I try to imagine this story as a fairy tale, something safely distant, something fabricated, but when I try to translate the present moment to a safe and fictional past, all I come up with is the sky on a clear night, full of falling stars.

. . .

We are always baking—in the middle of the summer, in the middle of the night. We are always making sure that when the men arrive they are offered something sweet.

One night I tell the witch I am starting to forget their names. The rooms are full then empty so fast, time seems to move vertically. One morning I walk in to bathe a man, and when I see his form on the bed, it is undefined, as if I am seeing him through tearing eyes. I see the form there on the bed, a man, but what I really see is several men transposed, all the men who've lived and left there on that bed, all the men whose bodies I've known. The man whose tongue swelled until he couldn't breathe. The man whose tears contained blood.

I cannot know, but I believe it will get worse before it gets better. And for all our insistence on remembering the past, this is one story I'd like to relegate to once upon a time.

The phone rings and I answer, but this time I know. This time I do not say, Hello? I am on the line and I hear the stuttered breathing, and I try to will the voice to speak. We both hold steady, in a stand-off of silence. Then I break it. What is it? I ask the voice. I hear the breathing on the other line, and if I close my eyes and trick myself into believing, I imagine the person is in the room with me and I feel their breath on my face. What are you trying not to say? I ask the monster, and then it is I who hangs up.

As I am giving him a sponge bath, a man who was once a computer programmer tells me about the best lover he ever had, biting his thumbnail the whole time. He tells it comically, in detail but also with exaggeration. It's a good story, the kind of story my brother and his friends used to tell me when I would visit him in the city. I can feel in his body the longing and nostalgia he has for the life he's left behind. I can feel in the skin around his bones that this body I am cleaning was once a body that inaugurated desire. Then he is done and we both give one last smile, not at each other but at the memory of that life. There is just the sound of my cloth softly wiping his skin and the sound of him biting the nail of his thumb until I put my hand around his and pull it away from his mouth. He looks at me. I'm not a good person, he says. I start to interject—I'm not a good person, he says more loudly. He seems to want to say more, but I don't push him. I am learning that half of my work is to be an ear to the mouths that will soon be gone.

It is easy to forget, but stories need not always have a purpose. We are quick to say that folktales have a moral or a lesson or a creed.

But most of the stories that have survived the ages are told for one purpose only, and that purpose is to say this: "Being human is difficult. Here is some evidence."

...

At night I walk the plots. I walk the plots and say a kind word at each spot, wonder how many more we will fill. I walk the plots until I come to my brother's, which I have marked with our nautilus fossil. But a strange thing has overcome me recently. I cannot find sorrow. There is only an anger so overwhelming, I become nauseous. So I sit where the fresh soil mounds, and I look up at the galaxy above.

One day I hope the witch will enter the story in another form, where it will be revealed how good she is. Where we will have to rewrite the story such that the world knows there are marvels if you look hard enough: in the wood and on the street. She won't lead us out of the labyrinth, but she does her part to quell its hurt. She gives the men beds. She gives the men drugs. She puts her lips on the men's foreheads.

We cannot know how this will end, but I read the fear in her face. And this morning, when she sent me on this task, I saw the first signs of defeat. We are in her ancient truck, me driving, her daughter in the passenger's seat. We are moving along the country roads, driving across state borders and over and through the hours. We are vigilant for the signs that say YARD SALE.

The witch's daughter takes the task of searching for the signs seriously. She is looking out the window, and when I glance at her, I think: What will she remember of this plague when she is older? Will she remember at all? Or will this plague still loiter in our blood, so that it is not past but present?

Then she spots one—a sign—and I tell her good work and I carefully tousle her hair. I pull the truck over and I am thinking: Will the children four generations from hers come to know this story? Or will it dissolve into history, so that they know it only as another bygone event?

We get out of the car. It's a good one—a rich assortment of the recycled refuse of a home. There are tables lining the yard. There are live oaks looming on the periphery of the property, and the Spanish moss moves in the wind. There is the sound of cicadas in the field beyond and it's getting to be dusk. I look out over the property, beyond the tables of wares, and I see an empty and abandoned sandbox. Just then, the witch's daughter takes my hand, and when she does, my whole body throbs once with a surge of grief and nostalgia. A heavy woman approaches, wrapping a wet cloth around her neck. She nods and smiles at us, and it is clear she is the owner of the home. Y'all lookin' for anything specific? she asks. Before I can speak, the witch's daughter says: Cookie jars.

Here is the last story my brother told me, and it is a story that's true: A man who was not ill took his ill lover to the Deep South, where the man had grown up. When they arrived, he carried his ill lover to his childhood bedroom and laid him on his childhood bed. The ill lover, a man who was once an actor, said the bed was the most comfortable bed his frame had ever known. The lover smiled wider than the man had seen in months, smiled and breathed deeply and shook his head. This bed, the lover said, his tongue caught in the cogs of thought and teeth. Here. I could end. This bed! Right here.

After the visit was over, the lovers, one sick, one well, went back to The Big Apple. But the mother. My god, that mother. The story is not done.

One day toward the end of the ill lover's life, there came a knock on the door. When the man who was still well opened it, both were astonished to see the childhood bed. The mother had traveled north with the bed so that the sick lover could spend his last days in it. And that is what happened; the following evening, the sick lover took his last breath in the bed, and the man held his mother fast. She kissed his wet cheeks and pulled his face away from hers and told him what I am trying to tell you here—that there are two kinds of labyrinths: those you are born into and must escape, and those you choose to enter in search of what lies inside.

| 1378 | 1456 | 1531 | 1605 | 1682 | **1759** | 1835 |
| 1910 | 1986 | 2061 | **2136** | **2211** | 2286 | 2365 |

EPISODES TOWARD AN ELEGY FOR HALLEY'S COMET

1759

The arms of a galaxy spin outward, crafting a spiral that coils according to a universal law. A spiral with the same dimensions is found in a spider's web.

2211

Two space probes disseminate the following: 01010011 01101111 01101111 01101110 00100000 01110100 01101000 01100101 00100000 01100011 01101000 01101001 01101100 01100100 01110010 01100101 01101110 00100000 01100010 01100101 01100011 01100001 01101101 01100101 00100000 01110100 01101111 01110100 01100001 01101100 01101100 01111001 00100000 01101100 01101111 01110011 01110100 00100000 01101001 01101110 00100000 01110100 01101000 01100101 00100000 01100111 01110010 01100101 01100001 01110100 00100000 01110111 01101001 01101100 01100100 01100101 01110010 01101110 01100101 01110011 01110011 00101110

Translated it reads: " . . . Soon the children became totally lost in the great wilderness . . ."

2136

The water carrier knows her efforts to help those left is in vain. But she still carries the water twice a day, and when she places the ladle against their lips, she sees their eyes close and their breathing slow. And while she knows she cannot fix their ruined earth—while she knows she is facing her extinction—she also knows it is easier to cope if she has a chore. It is easier to understand the storms that divide the ground as though it were clay, the fires that ash everything in their paths, the lightning that never ceases, when she is focused on a single task: the work of quenching thirst.

1759

The law that dictates the shape of the galaxy's spinning also dictates the aloe plant's spiral spikes. In a warm territory, a seed finds ground and time passes until the whorl begins. When it has matured, the plant is plucked and its seeping ooze soothes skin that is hot to the touch.

2136

The water carrier is at her river. She puts her hand into the moving water and pulls a palmful to her face. It is cold and awakens in her a brief moment of calm. Despite everything, there is still water. Water, she thinks, and pulls more toward her, letting it run down her face and arms, pooling it against her chest. She stands and breathes and walks into the river. Water, she thinks, and stretches her arms out, sees the river move between her fingers and legs. She shudders to think about what might happen if somehow there was not this.

It is the sound that disturbs her most. The world refuses to stay quiet. It thunders and groans and cracks. It weeps and wails and hums. Sometimes, at night, when dark pervades, she thinks the earth sounds human.

2211

The space probes disseminate: 01001001 01100110 00100000
01101000 01100101 01101100 01110000 00100000 01100100
01101001 01100100 00100000 01101110 01101111 01110100
00100000 01100011 01101111 01101101 01100101 00100000
01110011 01101111 01101111 01101110 00101100 00100000
01110100 01101000 01100101 01111001 00100000 01110111
01101111 01110101 01101100 01100100 00100000 01110000
01100101 01110010 01101001 01110011 01101000 00101110
00100000

It reads: " . . . If help did not come soon, they would perish . . ."

1759

A human pupil contracts after having been dilated. The curves of the nerves in the cornea follow the law of the galaxy's arms, the aloe's spiral, the path of an owl as it approaches its prey.

2136

The water carrier is fully clothed, wet and resting on a rock in the middle of the river. She is haunted by the images she saw two full moons ago, when she became lost and happened upon the ruins of a long-dilapidated house. When she opened the codex, she found inside sheets with markings and images that seemed to convey a tale. The images told of two siblings, but the angle seemed odd. It was as though the trees were telling the story of what unfolded beneath them, as though the canopy were narrating the tale.

It had given her a peculiar sensation, one of dread laced with hope. Maybe the trees are watching them now, the water carrier thinks. Maybe the world has its own language with which it composes our story. She is in the middle of the river on a rock and she looks around her at the moving water. Maybe we aren't the authors of our own end but minor players in a much more cosmic tale.

1759

A tropical storm develops. It winds its way in circles as it gathers speed. The path the wind travels echoes the shape of a moth's flight toward light, the bands in the human eye, water's path when it disperses from a spinning ball.

2136

The water carrier is sitting in the middle of her river. She is thinking that she is infinitesimal when she senses something is not right. She watches the water spin and swirl and slip away. Something is not right, she thinks. She rises.

2211

The probes: 01001101 01101001 01100100 01100100 01100001
01111001 00100000 01110100 01101000 01100101 00100000
01100011 01101000 01101001 01101100 01100100 01110010
01100101 01101110 00100000 01100011 01100001 01101101
01100101 00100000 01110100 01101111 00100000 01100001
00100000 01101100 01101001 01110100 01110100 01101100
01100101 00100000 01101000 01101111 01110101 01110011
01100101 00100000 01100010 01110101 01101001 01101100
01110100 00100000 01100101 01101110 01110100 01101001
01110010 01100101 01101100 01111001 00100000 01101111
01100110 00100000 01100011 01100001 01101011 01100101
00100000 01100001 01101110 01100100 00100000 01110111
01101001 01101110 01100100 01101111 01110111 01110011
00100000 01101101 01100001 01100100 01100101 00100000
01101111 01100110 00100000 01100011 01101100 01100101
01100001 01110010 00100000 01110011 01110101 01100111
01100001 01110010 00101110

It reads: " . . . Midday the children came to a little house built entirely of cake and windows made of clear sugar . . ."

2136

Her river is running in the opposite direction. Her river is running in reverse. She has witnessed all kinds of implausible ruin, but this revelation makes her unsteady with disbelief. She sits down and hugs her legs.

She thinks: There are forces at work beyond her understanding. If such forces can shift the course of a river, what about the spinning of the Earth?

2211

01010111 01101001 01110100 01101000 00100000 01100001
00100000 01110011 01100001 01100100 00100000 01101000
01100101 01100001 01110010 01110100 00100000 01000111
01110010 01100101 01110100 01100101 01101100 00100000
01100110 01100101 01110100 01100011 01101000 01100101
01100100 00100000 01110100 01101000 01100101 00100000
01110111 01100001 01110100 01100101 01110010 00100000
01101001 01101110 00100000 01110111 01101000 01101001
01100011 01101000 00100000 01001000 01100001 01101110
01110011 01100101 01101100 00100000 01110111 01100001
01110011 00100000 01110100 01101111 00100000 01100010
01100101 00100000 01100010 01101111 01101001 01101100
01100101 01100100 00101110

" . . . With a sad heart, Gretel fetched the water in which Hansel
was to be boiled . . ."

1759

The fossilized remains of a nautilus shell sit beneath the ground. Its chambers follow the same pattern as the spiraling aloe, the bands of the galaxy, the nerves of the human eye. The dimensions of the whirling chambers advance at a rate equal to that of a hurricane's arms or a winged creature's descent.

The fossil sits tucked between layers of clay. It waits for the day it is plucked, cleaned of the soil that hugs it, and held by a pair of small hands.

The comet is returning, but no one knows, except Edmond Halley, dead these seventeen years. The comet is returning, this time to be branded with his name. After this visit, the world will know the comet rounds its course and returns, but no one knows this yet. And this is why, when it passes, no one is looking up.

2136

It is the eternal predicament of humankind to see only what it wants to, the water carrier thinks. Everything around her fades and fails. She could stop right here, but their thirst. She is compelled to quench it. Mouths, the water carrier thinks. Her story is full of mouths.

1378 **1456** 1531 1605 1682 1759 1835

1910 **1986** 2061 2136 **2211** 2286 2365

UNTIRING MACHINES

Two MEN LOCK TOGETHER in love, clasp like a shut locket. And after, one leads the other to the kitchen and they try it differently and again. Then they share a bar of chocolate and a shower. Now they are lying in bed, naked except for the sheet, the fan running high and loud. The man who rents the apartment is a dancer and when he asks the other man's name, he is met with a shake of the head. No names, the man says, and the dancer offers him a smile and the mouth of his dripping bottle of beer. When the dancer asks if the man can at least tell him what he does for a living, the man laughs and tosses his hair in a way that does nothing to keep it out of his eyes. I'm in technology. Specifically, programming. Language design and compiler construction. So essentially, the dancer says, your job is in every way the opposite of mine. The programmer smiles and shakes his head. You know, the programmer says, long ago a computer was not a machine but a person. Usually a woman. A woman who crunched numbers for long hours in huge rooms. The dancer sighs loudly and steals back his beer, says the world revolves too fast. They nod and look out the window, which is small and displays only the imperfectly aligned bricks of the wall in the adjacent building. When the dancer asks the programmer what he's doing in the city, the programmer says he's here on business. Top-secret business. Shut the shades, the programmer says, smiling, and I'll tell you all about it.

Five hundred and thirty years before this, a woman stands in her kitchen, sweating. She takes a deep drink of water and lets it run down her shirt, staining the front of her bodice dark. She is await-ing the arrival of her brother. She had heard he would be coming home to Mainz this evening and wants to ensure he has a hot meal. She pulls a rag from around her neck and wipes her dripping face, then runs it along the pane of her chest and rests it on her shoulder. Before he'd left for Strasbourg, while working on his invention in Hof Humbrecht, she had cooked for him like this. Long evenings in which she was forbidden to disturb him meant she had made many midnight meals. When her brother tried to explain to her what he had created, she hadn't understood. It had something to do with making things plural. It had something to do with making many duplications of the words that surfaced on a page. She had put the plate in front of him and she'd admired the way his hands grew glossy from the meat he tore before placing it on his tongue. She does not know it yet, but tonight, when he arrives, he will show her two scrolls that will change the course of human history. For now, she leans over a boiling pot and does not notice when several drops of sweat from her neck fall into the broth below.

The programmer has his hand in the dancer's hair, bodies spread on the bed, wrapped around each other. He pauses for a minute, not sure where to start. He tells the dancer perhaps it's best to begin with a story. Perhaps one way to start is like this: Because the Earth is ever-moving, when something falls, it does not follow a straight path down. Every fall happens on a plane that is curved because as an object descends, it is also moving forward, propelled by Earth's rotation. You may think an object that you drop is falling in a line toward Earth, but the laws of the universe are deceiving you. When the dancer objects, arguing that this isn't a story, the man say that it is. It even has a moral, he says: Our reality is governed by forces far stronger than we can understand.

Two hundred and twenty-five years after this, long after the Earth revolts and flood and famine eliminate every being on the green and blue sphere, two space probes linger on the edges of the Milky Way. Launched a century prior to offer proof of humankind, a virtual trace on the endlessness of space, the probes disseminate a feed of data. They do not know that they are all that's left of the beings who launched them.

In the corner of the Gutenberg kitchen, a spider casts her snare. Food, the woman thinks. She remembers when there wasn't so much on their table, especially in winter. This was when they were young, before she'd told Johannes the secret about their father. She remembers the sharpness of hunger, the way it pierced and prodded from inside, as though an invisible force was trying to get out. It was an ache that began in the head, then journeyed south to the core before slithering along each limb. She knew one way to address an empty stomach was by keeping it full of fluid, and so she would give her brother large mouthfuls of water to fill the void in his gut. She stirs the broth and tries to remember the feeling of being hollow, a rind of skin wrapped around organ and bone.

They are sitting up now. The programmer begins: Think of everything in our books and encyclopedias and our tapes and cassettes as a vast forest of information. Think of it as a kind of thicket of knowledge that has depth and that is disordered and multiple and fractured. Can you imagine this forest? The dancer tells him he can try, and he does, but it feels as though this man is speaking a different language. The programmer says he's developing a digital forest with virtual property. The plots for each bit of property are called pages and they are free. The idea is that everyone can access the forest and build on it, plant and tend the seeds. When the digital foliage has blossomed and flourished, it will be like accessing a whole other universe, and this is how communication will be revolutionized. The programmer's eyebrows are raised, waiting for the dancer's response, and the dancer has to hide his doubt. It sounds like science fiction, he tells the programmer, smoothing out the sheets. The programmer laughs and shakes his head. I promise it is fact.

The woman brings the ladle to her mouth, sips a bit of broth. She cannot know it yet, but when her brother comes tonight, he will unroll for her two scrolls. Each scroll will be encoded with the same set of markings. She won't have to ask him to decode them for her because he knows she cannot read them. He will clear his throat and his eyes will follow the lines of text and his voice will begin a tale she knows well—that of two siblings abandoned in the wood. This is the story she used to tell him, in the years when she was old enough to do the washing at the river with the women but young enough not to have started to bleed. She will look at the code on the page and watch his eyes consume it, and she will think: It is a kind of magic that a story lives in those strange shapes. She had gone to school and tried for years to learn the skill of decoding, but her brain miscalculated time and again, making of the clean line of words a complex, eddying net. And so tonight she will listen to her brother tell the story twice, one reading for each scroll, and then explain that this is what he has invented. She will look at him, then down again at each scroll until he sees she does not understand. He will stand behind her and whisper into her ear that one of them was done by a hand and the other a machine.

The probes contain the digital human footprint, a virtual catalog of life on Earth. This is how the known world—its bodies and bridges and thought and hugs and war, its bathtubs and software, its art and discord—is capsuled and encoded into every corner of the sky, and then beyond. The probes disseminate the information, which presses itself slim and spreads itself wide, folds and doubles back around and through itself. It moves like water through the ether, sliding and breaking and drilling a measureless core toward whatever comes next.

The dancer lies on the bed, looking up at the ceiling as the man goes on, describing a future world the dancer can only vaguely imagine. He gets bits and pieces of the narrative: It is called The Universal Forest. The Forest is simple and abstract enough so that others can build entirely as-yet unimagined experiences, extending its limits and boundaries. The Forest has no center so it can never be controlled. The Forest is navigated through different slides that have internal doors, permitting you to go inside and then inside again, as if it were a three-dimensional maze. The programmer pauses here, flips his hair, apologizes, noting that he's having trouble creating language to describe how to navigate this forking world. It will come in time, he says, but, too, I have the feeling I'm on a kind of ethereal clock. The dancer takes his beer back and swigs, wonders if he means this in more than one way. The programmer explains the problem: Ideas are promiscuous—they want to spread and they want to combine. The dancer offers him the bottle but the programmer refuses. I'm onto this thing, but I can't know if I'm going to be able to pull it off before someone else does, he tells the dancer. In fact, another team is working on a similar project, but they're calling their version The World Wide Web.

Her brother will show her the two identical scrolls and ask if she can tell the difference. She will lean in close with each and then step back. She will walk around the table, view the story upside down. She will think of the fact that for one version, a human hand made the curves of the letters, knuckles ink-stained and palm in pain. She will think that a man delicately swept his fingers over the page when it was done, that the work of scripting these words in their careful line caused hunger and fatigue. Does a machine grow tired? Can a machine ache?

All of it sounds like science fiction, the dancer thinks. Or folktale. It sounds like a beautiful myth. The Universal Forest, the dancer whispers. A new and disembodied world.

The woman wipes her forehead with a bit of cloth she keeps swung around her neck. The salt of the sweat gets in her eyes and stings. She does not know it yet, but tonight, after her brother has eaten and retired, as she is trying to fall asleep, she will think about the story of the siblings as it lies on each scroll. She can't decode the markings, but she remembers how she told it, and she finds it funny to think of the story she used to tell with her voice—a story that required a certain shift of tone in parts, a lift here and a nod there to ensure the audience understood what was left unsaid—all of that reduced to an encryption. She thinks of the story, the father who sends his son into the woods because of the way he desires. The sister who follows him for protection. The witch who takes them in and cares for them. When the father, full of regret, tries to come for them, the witch cooks him and the children eat him up.

Right now the woman is stirring her stew, but tonight she will lie her body flat and think of her own father and his ugly transgressions. Then she will think of this story, how it is about sibling union, about the power of children to overcome. It is about how, when our parents cut the cord of life, we survive, persist, and sometimes get revenge.

The programmer sits on the end of the bed, runs his hands around the now-empty bottle, letting the condensation saturate his palms. Sometimes I think about my niece and nephew, he says, how I can only vaguely imagine what the world will look like when they are grown. The dancer stands and starts to dress, wonders what his own sister would think of this man's ethereal universe. Like a fairy tale in one of the collections she studies, the dancer thinks. Or rather, like a horror story, the gothic architecture replaced by an intricately designed set of synapses that flicker and crack.

Soon her brother will ask her: Can you tell which is human-made and which is artificial? And she will think: What are words without a heart beating behind them?

The woman pulls a loaf of bread out of the fire, listens to the crust snap and click as it begins to cool. Twins were rare when they were young, and she recalls how the others in the village would ask to study their faces. She had often looked at him and imagined her own face transposed over his, a kind of comfortable mask. Gutenberg's sister wipes the sweat from her chest with her rag, looks at the finished table. When last she'd seen her brother, he had told her he was creating something that would change the world. The problem, he said, was that a book is too expensive when transcribed by human hands. This is why knowledge cannot be dispersed. What we need is an economical way to make the printed word public. What we need is an untiring machine that perpetually replicates. She had nodded, understood that part of invention is a bloated faith in the self. Part of creation, she thinks, slicing the bread, is making believe. She wipes her face with her rag and recalls a moment when they were young and running through the fields behind their home, running away from some imagined threat. They'd spent all day under the sun, and when they finally made it back home, the skin on her brother's neck was such that it puckered and bubbled and, days later, peeled. The skin of a potato is not unlike the skin of a man, she thinks, stirring the stew. She thinks of the story of two siblings, how the father could not love his son. How the witch fed the children their father and their hunger was satiated. She thinks about the sweet meat of a father on the lips, what it must feel like to pull the skin of a father off the bone, use the teeth to crush the father muscle, and push it down the throat with the tongue. Her father is one who might deserve that kind of end.

The probes disseminate their information into the vast expanse. They listen to the haunting sounds of space: the groan of winds that move at unparalleled speed; the thunder of young satellites finding their course; the clamor of two asteroids meeting, echoed infinitely. And amidst this cacophony, the probes dispense the proof that humans once were: language, rules, fear, nostalgia, mourning. Regret and affection. Hate. The information tumbles, the code coiling through and around and beyond. It extends toward an elsewhere of which the bodies on Earth could never have fully conceived.

We're at the opposite of the edge, the programmer says. He is staring out the window, speaking to the brick wall. What do you mean? the dancer asks from behind him on the bed. The programmer tells him that it's a rare time, that we're at the same place we were when we realized the world was round. We're using the same internal code of curiosity engrained in our veins that once pushed our species to keep roaming the world. It's that tendency we have to look at a vista in admiration, but just a beat afterward wonder what lies beyond.

The dancer crawls toward the programmer, who sits on the edge of the bed, and when he reaches him, the dancer sets his chin on the programmer's shoulder. Breadcrumbs, the dancer says, and the programmer looks at him, confused. To navigate The Forest. Use breadcrumbs, the dancer says. The programmer breathes in deeply and exhales, nods his head. Then together they look out the window and study the wall.

The woman thinks of her twin, the way they are two but also, strangely, one. The cord of flesh that makes her navel broke and branched and made his, too. This is why, after they'd been sent off to school and she'd had time to understand the brand of wrong her father had inflicted on her, she told her brother what he'd done. And her brother believed her, held her tight, and whispered that there were evils in the world and together they would navigate around them. They'd never returned for a holiday, instead spent them with cousins of their mother, and their father had left it at that. Neither spoke of their father again, though on cold nights, the fire cracking, they would tell stories about their mother, gone when they were still small: her cool hand on their faces when they were sick, her thin fingers tracing images on their backs in the bath, her whispers waking them in the morning before the sun rose. The woman wipes the sweat from her forehead, then runs the rag along her chest. She has no one but Johannes, she thinks, since her father ruined her. It is only Johannes she has, and she is proud of him. And then the woman thinks a funny thing. No one can know if he will be remembered for any of his inventions, but if by chance his likeness becomes the face of greatness, within its shape she will be present, too.

The probes offer their feed to the indefinite elsewhere for years and decades and centuries, until they stop calculating time. And just when they begin to think their voices are in vain, on the surface of a world uncanny in its likeness to Earth, a receiver picks up their feed.

The man kisses the top of the dancer's head. He says: If I'm ever in the city again—but the dancer waves him off. Be careful out there, the dancer says, and they both know what that means. Then he says: I'll see you in The Forest.

After the man is gone, the dancer runs a hot bath, strips, and enters the tub. When he was too young to understand, his sister once did this for him—drew the water far hotter than their mother would allow—and told him this is what it means to feel pleasure. He remembers the hot enveloping the organ of his skin as strange, at once an ache and a comfort. He dries himself, dresses, and walks to the studio, observing the varied shape of the clouds. It is as he's looking up at those ethereal shapes that he thinks of his sister. He remembers the tale that she told him about the siblings lost in the woods, how they were sent out because their parents could not feed them but defeated a witch and made it back home. He remembers the metaphor of the breadcrumbs, how his sister explained to him the strangeness of the fact that this is what most people know about the story. The thing is, she'd said—and he is just now remembering it, too late, he is thinking now—the breadcrumbs don't lead them home. It's the breadcrumbs most people remember, but the breadcrumbs fail. The dancer realizes his mistake, thinks he should try to track down the programmer and explain. But how to track down a man without a name in a city of seven million? He walks and thinks and regrets and soon he finds himself in front of the studio, reading a note on the door that says rehearsal is canceled though, it seems, the door isn't locked.

He is at the studio now, moving his frame in a very careful pattern, the muscles in his head coordinating with the muscles in his body, computing how to discipline his form. He bends and morphs his bones, shifts swiftly, his core an axis, his limbs satellites. This is how he memorizes the choreography. He repeats the routine over and over, twenty, forty times, his heart beating to some new rhythm until time is lost and he is just a vortex of particles made infinitely plural in the studio's mirrors.

In each of these pasts and futures, in each of these moments on, beyond, and after the globe, the comet follows its orbit, every swing around the sun and to the end of the universe another lap on a cosmic track. It wonders what it means to live a life that is not bound by law. But then, each consciousness on every orb the comet passes is also locked into its place, sutured to the rind of its world, even if it thinks that it is not.

Gutenberg is nearing the house in which his sister waits. In his hands are two renderings of her favorite story, about the siblings who are cast out. He is thinking about his twin sister, how even after all these years to look into her face and see himself smiling back both comforts and unsettles him. To look into the face of his sister is a kind of coming home, though home here means more a time than a place. He is thinking that their mother never told them who was born first. He approaches the house and he can smell the meal she's cooking. He reaches for the door handle and breathes deep, happy for the miracle of food and fire and family. He can hear his sister's steps approach from the other side.

No one alive knows who was born first, and so no one knows in which body he dwells—the original or the copy.

| 1378 | 1456 | 1531 | 1605 | 1682 | 1759 | 1835 |
| 1910 | 1986 | 2061 | 2136 | 2211 | 2286 | 2365 |

EPISODES TOWARD AN ELEGY FOR HALLEY'S COMET

2211

Two space probes disseminate the following: 01010100 01101000
01100101 00100000 01110111 01101001 01110100 01100011
01101000 00100000 01110100 01101111 01101100 01100100
00100000 01000111 01110010 01100101 01110100 01100101
01101100 00100000 01110100 01101111 00100000 01100111
01100101 01110100 00100000 01101001 01101110 00100000
01110100 01101000 01100101 00100000 01101111 01110110
01100101 01101110 00101100 00100000 01100010 01110101
01110100 00100000 01000111 01110010 01100101 01110100
01100101 01101100 00100000 01110011 01100001 01110111
00100000 01110111 01101000 01100001 01110100 00100000
01110011 01101000 01100101 00100000 01101000 01100001
01100100 00100000 01101001 01101110 00100000 01101101
01101001 01101110 01100100 00101110

Translated, it reads: " . . . The witch told Gretel to get in the oven,
but Gretel saw what she had in mind . . ."

1910

The nurse untwists and lifts the top of the cookie jar, peers inside. The comet has not yet come, and she has just learned the illustrator has disappeared from the Asylum. The nurse knows the illustrator must have left something in the cookie jar for her. She sees a collection of paper and she hesitates, imagining what the pages might contain. She does not know that these pages hold a story that will outlive humankind. All she knows is that in this moment, the jar is full of possibility.

The nurse pauses. She holds the cookie jar in her hands, registers the weight of the vessel. The glass is cool and smooth and promising, she thinks. What has this jar held in its past?

The nurse thinks: What will the jar contain in its future?

1456

Johannes Gutenberg's legs are stretched across his sister's lap. She has wrapped his feet in blankets and propped them in front of the fire. She is telling him the story of the siblings, the same story that lives on the scrolls he showed her earlier tonight. She has a way of telling, he thinks, and he closes his eyes as she narrates the tale.

Before she'd told him what their father had done, she had told several others but no one believed her. No one had listened, sat her down and wiped her brow and opened their ears to her tale. But when she told him, it changed the lens through which he viewed his past. Everything seemed instantly transparent, when before it had donned a guise. To his sister Johannes had listened and because he had listened, he eventually believed.

His invention is for her, and all those who need a way to tell their stories. It is for every sister who once had a story that went unbelieved. When people ask him what he's invented, he tells them this: a device that will make the world listen.

She stops her story and he keeps his eyes closed, waiting for her to go on. They are at the moment when the siblings have come to the house made of sweets. He waits but there is only silence as she conjures suspense. She has him in her power with her story, holds him captive in the middle of her tale.

1682

Edmond Halley has asked his niece to tell him a story. Tell me a story about a comet, he has asked and watched the vapor of his breath. Now, his niece looks up at him and he sees that there is something in her face, something that tells him she is about to cast a spell. She looks otherworldly, he thinks, a kind of ethereal energy exuding from her frame. She opens her mouth to speak and stops for a moment before she begins, breathes in with her teeth and lips parted, as though her story doesn't want to be told. She breathes and he shivers when he sees that no vapor leaves her mouth.

1835

The Brothers Grimm have written down the tale. They have committed it to paper, and confirmed this is how it will live.

It is Jacob's breathing that concerns Wilhelm. Jacob is breathing deeply and his eyes seem glossed. He rises and goes to his brother, pulls him from his chair. Jacob, Wilhelm thinks, this is my Jacob, and he holds his brother fast.

2211

01000111 01110010 01100101 01110100 01100101 01101100
00100000 01110010 01100001 01101110 00100000 01110100
01101111 00100000 01001000 01100001 01101110 01110011
01100101 01101100 00100000 01100001 01101110 01100100
00100000 01110101 01101110 01101100 01101111 01100011
01101011 01100101 01100100 00100000 01101000 01101001
01110011 00100000 01100100 01101111 01101111 01110010
00101110

" . . . Gretel ran to Hansel and unlocked his door . . ."

2136

The water carrier looks behind her at the river that runs in reverse. She respects the forces that have made such change possible. She looks at the river, then up at the trees, further on and into the sky. Her ears and mind are open, waiting to hear the earth narrate what will happen next.

1456

I'm listening, Johannes Gutenberg tells his sister.

1682

I'm listening, Edmond Halley tells his niece.

1835

I'm listening, Wilhelm Grimm whispers to his brother, and kisses the side of his head.

1378

Gretel holds Hansel in her arms. She wants to tell him that she hears him, but she cannot mouth the words. She holds her brother close and listens to the air move through the trees.

There is an archive of alternate endings, she tells him, and every one ends differently than this.

2211

01000001 01101100 01101100 00100000 01110100 01101000
01100101 01101001 01110010 00100000 01100011 01100001
01110010 01100101 01110011 00100000 01110110 01100001
01101110 01101001 01110011 01101000 01100101 01100100
00101100 00100000 01100001 01101110 01100100 00100000
01110100 01101000 01100101 01111001 00100000 01101100
01101001 01110110 01100101 01100100 00100000 01101000
01100001 01110000 01110000 01101001 01101100 01111001
00100000 01110100 01101111 01100111 01100101 01110100
01101000 01100101 01110010 00101110 10000000011101

" . . . Then all their cares vanished, and they lived happily together."

2365

1986

Breadcrumbs, the dancer says, his chin on the programmer's shoulder. To navigate The Universal Forest. The programmer thinks for a moment, bites his thumbnail.

If you find yourself on the wrong path, follow the breadcrumbs back.

1378 1456 1531 1605 1682 1759 1835

1910 1986 **2061** 2136 2211 2286 2365

HANSEL'S LAMENT

Our mother and father don't meet. We are the *déjà vu* that comes to them at the precipice of waking. When they rise in their separate lives, we are the vague and formless haunting that they do not speak of to their respective lovers in the kitchen over coffee. We are that phantom something they qualify as nightmare and forget.

Our father's house does not burn down when he is young because he remembers to turn off the gas range. And so we have photos of him from youth, and he retains his witty charm, and his mother does not hold his mistake over him when she wants to implement harm. And because the house does not burn down, we spend holidays in it, and know the corridors and nooks by feel, and see our faces populating the walls, and it is not a mythic place that registers in our childhood as a blazing labyrinth but a familiar and welcome structure. And our father does not live the rest of his life in fear of fires. And our father does not have to forgive himself because there is no event in our family history for which he should be forgiven.

And you and I don't live a life linked but also severed. And we don't give each other bruises and say ugly things that cannot be unsaid and betray each other's trust. And you do not let me sneak into your bed when our parents are fighting, the sound of broken dishes and screams muted by the towel you shove along the bottom of your bedroom door. And I don't admire you so much and seek your approval and you don't ignore me and sneak me beer. In fact, I stay off the drink forever. I never take a sip.

Our mother does not get mind-sick because her father does not die when she is in her early teens because the doctors catch the cyst. And so she does not tell us when we are young how important it is to create. And she does not spend her days reading us books and watching our performances, because she is capable of working and wants a career. And she wears high heels and she works out and cooks elegant meals and our house is clean. And she does not tell us to invest in mystery and she does not tell us to respect hurt.

I don't find myself in with a bad crowd because our father never tells me to be a man—instead he lets me be a boy. And so I do not tell you that spring evening just how low I am willing to go, and you don't spend twelve hours convincing me this is not my destined route. And when dawn climbs over the rolling hills of the backyard of the house that we didn't move from because our parents were turned down for that loan, I do not tell you that you have changed me infinitely, exponentially, that in this single evening you were every sketched figure I'd ever imagined would save me.

And our father does not cast out our uncle. Our father does not tell us that it is because our uncle and he had a falling-out. And we don't learn years later that our uncle was ill and our father refused to help him so that he died alone at a stranger's house in the South.

And we do not try to find his remains, and learn no one is left who knows where he is buried. No: instead, our father takes our uncle in and cares for his only sibling, tends his weeping sores and rubs his back when he is sick from medication. And we are there to read to him the stories he read us, and we let him flip the pages. And our uncle gets well and finds love and grows grey and stops biting his nails and when we're older, we drink iced tea in my backyard. And he teaches you bad words in other languages. And you teach him how to beat me at pool.

All that is possible—all that unfolds—because our mother does not find out that you are pregnant. Our mother does not find this out and tell our father, and they don't sit you down one evening and tell you that they want you out. And I don't pack the car and check the oil and fill the tank and go with you. And this is how we do not travel south, the two of us on a course toward a new life. And on the second day of driving, we don't run into a storm on the winding roads of the Appalachians and we don't crash. And because we do not crash, because we do not travel to the southern states because our parents do not cast you out, your body is not broken and your mind does not turn off and therefore, you are not killed. And your fifteen years walking this planet do not become the only years you do, and so you are not all memory to me now. And I do not go on, first measuring days and then months, until by some cruel logic I become older than you. And my skin is not tattooed with your name and I don't spend the decades watching that name fade as my skin sags and thins and grows covered in age spots. And I don't build and ruin things and fear and love without you and my body does not grow while yours decays beneath Earth's crust. And you do not haunt me like a riddle with no reply. No—instead—those keys go missing or the car is never purchased or the car is never built.

In fact, there are no cars at all, because there is no revolution that makes them simple to manufacture, because we do not dig beneath the earth for the liquid remains of organic matter dead for millions of years. And there are no paved roads connecting the northern states to the southern states. And an auto-mobile is merely the stuff of science fiction.

In fact, there are no southern states because the North and South are not one because the South wins sovereignty. And with it all degrees of tragedy that manifest in plural ways.

No, in truth, our country is not discovered, persists as ocean on maps for years, and the people who live here are a secret the land keeps.

In fact, there is not an Earth, because the chemicals that intercourse to formulate the majesty that is our world miss their temporal assembling. And because there is no Earth, there is no force pulling the solar system into its careful order and there is nothing to orbit, so the moon is not a satellite but just another body of rock moving within the murky logic of space.

And because there is not an Earth because there is not a collision that harnesses and perpetrates everything we know as fact, there is not a universe in the way that we would define one. There is only a series of duplications and shatterings, a perpetual unpleating, a sequence of rupturing cusps. There is only a great vacancy we navigate as light.

And the abstraction qualified as me tumbles and shuttles outside the dimension of time toward the shapeless entity that is you, and together we work to illuminate the void in which we dwell.

And on the surface of an elsewhere, a child points to a brightness in the sky and asks how it began.

1378 1456 1531 1605 1682 1759 1835

1910 1986 2061 2136 2211 2286 2365

THE TERRESTRIAL DILEMMA

Hansel asks: Is this how it begins? He points up to the night sky toward the vivid smear, an illumination that looks like the trail of a fast-traveling fire. We both forget the question, enfolded in the strange affair above. When I feel most alone, I remember I am part of the cosmos, a celestial event. We are part of a system, for better and for worse.

Gretel tells me there are crueler fates than being abandoned in the wood. But we've been here several moons now and I am growing thin: my patience, my waist. My mind gets away from me by the time the sun is low, and I start to imagine the peace that comes with being finished. I imagine our bodies have run out of life and rest forever in the brush, dissolving until all that is left is the framework. Each day this seems more possible, and so each day I grow closer to telling her the secret I've kept buried in my bones.

He can never know, but this is our mother's doing. The truth is she has come to believe she cannot mother a son like him. I saw the plotting in the way she held her form; I read the wrong all through her body. And so when she told him to attend to the fictional task she had crafted in the wood, I said I would accompany him. When she protested, I placed my hand upon her hand and this is how she learned I knew her plot. It has to be some new brand of maliciousness to lead the two beings a mother held inside her for three turns of the year on a strange path into the night to be forever gone. Hansel thought it was an adventure, and I let him. Boys are easy to deceive, our mother told me once. This is why she sent us toward tomorrow's end while Father was away, as if to prove a man is just a boy with more to lose.

> This happened once before, and I brought pebbles to ensure we knew our route back home. I dropped them and they made the way back simple. Gretel was proud because she said I had used sharp thinking quickly, and this was something to be praised. But this time I could not gather pebbles—I could only grab a loaf of bread. It was heavy in my satchel, and I was careful to drop the bits so that they were still large. The pebbles had been white; the bread was black, and I worried we might not see the ripped portions in the dark.

I could have told him don't bother when I saw him drop the first crumb, but the truth is that I need him to believe. I need him to cleave to possibility. That the birds and beasts of the forest were trailing us at a careful pace, devouring the bread and following us further into the abyss—this I left unsaid. This is his first encounter with the real, and he needs to meet it gently. When on our first route he had dropped the pebbles and we made our way back home, I thought our mother might reconsider. But I have come to learn her heart is anchored to her hate.

A story, Gretel says, to pass the time. And so I begin a tale. It must be epic in size in order to last the days. It must in some ways not end, so that we can stretch it to fit our particular needs. Gretel says this is how the best stories are told, with enough space to make them say several things at once.

His story begins in a city and involves two loving brothers, united as tightly as we. This strikes me as cunning because he has always loved symmetry. In the end, this might ruin him.

I set the story in a city and I tell her it is about siblinghood and stolen voices, stories that are ripped from villager's tongues. To make it more troubling, I decide to tell it in a manner not about the past or the present, but about what will be. A pair of brothers will traverse the land stealing stories, I tell her. The brothers will take the stories from the mouths of the people of the hills and the valleys and the villages. They will record the stories on bound scripts for distribution. It will be a time when these scripts are dispensed in great numbers, and this is how the voices will live on. The brothers will trap the people's voices, and then release them into eras far beyond our own. The tale comes easy and I realize that in crafting this narrative, I am a manager of fear. It is not a secret that my character is tender, but in this moment I feel brave, as though my flesh is glass.

Because I taught him how to weave a story, and because I know him better than he is ready to know himself, I see how the story will end. That he has used a tense that designates the future means it will haunt better, more effectively. I once told him that strong stories link risk and desire. In some ways, he is my fault.

I tell her that the brothers live to capture and steal the stories, then brand them with their shared name. But by capturing, they pollute them. Instead of permitting the stories to bend and fold with each new teller, the scripts are like coffins that calcify the tales. I look at her and she is keeping her gaze forward, trying to hide her fear. I see her run her tongue along her top lip, her private sign for concern. What is it that compels her to feel she must protect me?

I have seen his face in the market, in the village, at the school. I have seen his face fall upon other faces and have seen the way it shifts with want. I am his fierce protector, but when I see him in these moments—his lips growing slack in a way they used to when he was young and I would wash his hair, move my fingertips in slow loops across his skull—I grow nervous. It is in these moments I know he is someone I can never fully guard. What I see there is what has installed disgust in our mother: a longing for bodies shaped like his.

But one day, I tell her, the brothers hear a narrative that seems to echo their own. It is about two siblings, an elder and a younger. And because I know good stories contain tension at every turn, I take a chance. I tell her that the story echoes their own because it is about two siblings who are abandoned and grow lost in the wood. I glance up, and there is that brilliant stain across the sky. Gretel has taught me that the strongest stories join risk with desire. She cannot know I know how true that is.

He wants me to speak, and as much as I want to caution him of the labyrinth ahead, I need to let him use his own lips. I am trying to teach him to be someone who is vocal about his hurt.

She is silent, and the pause is making me waver. Does speaking a feeling make it a fact? She told me once that language is opaque, a very elegant concealing. But I am starting to think it is a prism, and if I can maneuver it just right, the light will amplify and liberate the truth.

Mother once pulled me aside. Don't let him lean that way, she told me. I shook my head at the ground. All speech is a code, I thought. She cradled the back of my head and pulled my face close to hers. I've heard of an inoculation, an antidote, she said—and I reeled back to exhibit my revulsion. She let go of me, sighed loudly, nodded once. This will break your father, she said, and I: You broke him before we were born.

If the guilt and longing were not so intimately bound, if they were not in essence the same feeling, I would not delay the saying. But I am growing in these woods. I can feel them working on me like a dark elixir, all my confessions collecting along the rim of my mouth. I am starting to wonder if we will get out unscathed.

I don't stop him because I am collecting myself. I am looking at the world beyond, above, thinking of the way the day dissolves. I am trying to teach him to carry his pain discreetly. Could it be that I am wrong?

There are skills that are practical—building wagons, tending garden, baking pastries, cobbling shoes—but Gretel always told me the skill to practice most is storytelling. Those who are trained in the art of telling have a certain kind of power that other artisans do not. A good story can wind a man around your finger, make him give you what you want. I am not alone in the village, in the valley. There are others like me, and because I know that speech is a code, we use it very carefully. I want to tell Gretel that I have known the inside of mouths and the curves of lower backs and the muscles of shoulders. I have known the skin that never meets the sun. I want to tell Gretel that I am not alone, and more than that I want to tell Gretel, neither is she.

That we are united in our venture and in our siblinghood—that we are bound to each other by the womb that we shared—should offer great solace and comfort. But as our bodies grow into their shape and our thoughts become hardened, we also grow apart and independent. I am not wise, but I am prudent enough to know this is a trial for all siblings and beyond—that all people who stand on our ground and look up to the same sun are both bound together and yet navigate this troubled world alone. Once I believed this was a law of nature, one that operated also in the sky. But lately I have come to learn the truth: It is a terrestrial dilemma.

What I know about stories concerned with what will come is that they harbor possibility. There is always the lingering notion of perhaps. And this is why I say it: The story the brothers steal is about a boy who desires uncommonly and the mother who sends him into the woods. The story is about this boy and his sister, who would not abandon him. I tell her this story will come to be heard by bodies and minds in eras that are not yet dreamed of. I tell her that this narrative will be told through modes we can only vaguely grasp. The brothers will steal this tale and deploy it long after this evening ends, I tell her, and she grabs my hand.

What is story if not the safe harbor for our most disturbing imaginings? I learned early that the notion of what will come to pass haunts better. But, too, it is about the storyteller—who you choose to trust and why. From where comes your decision to believe the breath that leaves the mouth that tells.

> Gretel holds my hand and I look up at the canopy of trees, learn the way the branches network far above us. It reminds me of the spider thread that forms an intricate web in the corners of our room. The wounded cannot know they will linger there until they are fetched. They do not know their fate before they choose to put a foot upon the thread. I have heard that boys are easy to deceive. I am here to say that they are not.

We shape reality around the forms that fit. How will his story end? We tell stories in order to share and to warn, and in his I have found myself caught. For it was I who taught him the best way to trap a listener is to make her desire beyond the story's close.

> Just as I am beginning to tell about how the brothers end our tale, I see we have come upon a house. It is handsome, doll-like, and my eyes have tricked me into believing that it is made of sweets. I want to be treated to it, my gut empty, but Gretel, she warns me. She has told me forever what it means to take the route along the river versus the one that curves and breaks between the trees. I am interested in transgression, she knows. She knows—I see it in her when she licks a thumb to remove dirt from my cheek. She knows, and when I see her look at me that way, I know, too—I know that she will save me. What I don't know is who will save her.

We have come upon a house that I see is also a trap. Hansel's pace quickens with anticipation and he relays to me how it is constructed of every kind of saccharine thing, but all I see is a prison. I try to warn him, but boys are easy to deceive. I look up at the sky and when I squint it looks like the smear may be a broken star. Hansel is my companion, but he is also my charge. I have walked this world and learned its ugly rules and tried to impart in him understanding. I can't know what will happen, but I know each hour is an ultimately solitary venture. When I feel most alone, I remember I am part of the cosmos, a celestial event. I know we are part of a system, a story. What I don't know is: Are you, too?

ACKNOWLEDGMENTS

This book borrows and reimagines documented material from the lives of the following: Johannes Gutenberg, Edmond Halley, Jacob and Wilhelm Grimm, Ruth Coker Burks.

Portions of this book previously appeared (in sometimes radically different form) in the following publications:

"Of Breadcrumbs and Constellations" in *Michigan Quarterly Review*; "Circumnavigations" in *West Branch*; "Episodes Toward an Elegy for Halley's Comet" in *TriQuarterly*; "The Marvelous Spiral" (as "Lifespan of Halley's Comet") in *New Delta Review*; "Untiring Machines" in *Slice*; "Hansel's Lament" (as "The Archive of Alternative Endings") in *Hayden's Ferry Review*.

Thank you to:

Richard Powers. Ander Monson. Laird Hunt. Bret Lott.

Emily Forland. Dan Wickett. Steve Gillis.

Ralph Crispino, Jr. Joanne Paradis. The I-Park Foundation.

Ron Drager. Valerie Drager. Leland Drager.

Michelle Dotter. Michelle Dotter. Michelle Dotter. Michelle Dotter. Michelle Dotter. Michelle Dotter. Michelle Dotter. Michelle Dotter. Michelle Dotter. Michelle Dotter. Michelle Dotter. Michelle Dotter.

Allan G. Borst.

ABOUT THE AUTHOR

Lindsey Drager is the author of *The Sorrow Proper*, winner of the 2016 John Gardner Fiction Award, and *The Lost Daughter Collective*, winner of a 2017 Shirley Jackson Award and finalist for a Lambda Literary Award.